BACK-ALLEY SHOOT-OUT

Three big men suddenly loomed in front of her as Charity turned into a dark alley. One of the hardcases had a big Bowie.

Moving fast, Charity Rose drew her Colt Lightning and squeezed off a round. Yellow-orange muzzle-bloom reflected off the ten-inch blade as the man holding it stopped in his tracks. He stared at the female bounty hunter from three wet, black eyes; then the one between his eyebrows began to bleed. Charity triggered another shot. Hot lead bored into the hardcase's throat. Uttering a soft, gurgling wail, he back-pedaled a few steps and fell dead.

Recovering from their momentary shock, the two other men tried to unlimber their guns. Charity crouched and spun to one side as the owlhoot she faced shot quick and wide. His partner gave a surprised grunt and crumpled to the ground with a wound in the upper right section of his chest.

Without a second to spare, Charity rapid-fired hot lead into the gunsel's heart. He blinked, then began a gagging cough that brought up a gout of dark blood. His twitching body sank to the ground, the light fading quickly from his unseeing eyes.

WHITE SQUAW BY E. J. HUNTER

WHITE SQUAW #14   (2075, $2.50)

As Rebecca Caldwell and her trusted companion Lone Wolf are riding back to the Dakota Territory, their train is ambushed by angry Sioux warriors. Becky ultimately finds out that evil Grover Ridgeway is laying claim to the land that the Indians call their own — and decides to take Grover in hand and pump out some information. Once she has him firmly in line, the White Squaw blows the cover off of his operation!

WHITE SQUAW #18   (2585, $2.95)

Hot on the heels of her long-time enemy, Roger Styles, Rebecca Caldwell is determined to whip him into shape once and for all. Headed for San Antonio and eager for action, Becky's more than ready to bring the lowdown thieving Styles under thumb — especially when she discovers he's made off with her gold. Luck seems to be on the White Squaw's side when Styles falls into her lap — and ends up behind bars.

WHITE SQUAW #19   (2769, $2.95)

Rebecca Caldwell was in no mood for romance after owlhoots murdered her lover Bob Russel. But with the rich, handsome teamster, Win Harper, standing firm and coming on hard, Becky feels that old familiar fire rising up once more . . . and soon the red-hot halfbreed's back in the saddle again!

E.J. HUNTER

HEAD HUNTER

#8: NEVADA CLAIM STRIPPER

ZEBRA BOOKS
KENSINGTON PUBLISHING CORP.

Special acknowledgements to Mark K. Roberts

ZEBRA BOOKS

are published by

Kensington Publishing Corp.
475 Park Avenue South
New York, NY 10016

First printing: June, 1990

Printed in the United States of America

CHAPTER 1

Small white puffs dotted the soft blue dome over Sweetwater Creek, some twenty miles from Virginia City, Nevada Territory. Water burbled musically over smooth rocks and swirled in eddies that promised rich deposits of washed-out silver. Here, at the claim farthest upstream, a bonanza pocket of gold also had been discovered. Two prospectors worked the claim, chill water to midthigh, as they mucked out shovel loads of the bottom and dumped them in a long riffle box.

"How much you figger we've got now, Eb?" the younger asked his partner.

Eb paused to scratch behind one ear with a grimy finger. "Must be three—four hundred dollars worth, Max."

Max grinned and overturned another shovel of gravel and mud. "Not bad for only four days. Not like the big strikes ten year ago, but handsome all the same. When we take it in?"

"*We* ain't gonna do it," Eb answered. "What with those claim-jumpers hanging around, someone's got to stay here and guard our stake. We'll take turns goin' to town and stayin' here. 'Sides, when we do take in our first load, this area'll be swarmin' with fellers lookin' to hit it rich, too."

They went back to work, bending, dipping and pouring. Fifteen minutes passed in the serenity of this hilly country; birds twittered in the trees, squirrels hastened to store away the last of their supplies for winter. Suddenly the small creatures around the creek went silent. Eb paused and looked around. A crow cursed him and took flight. Eb swore back, then again began shoveling gravel.

A trio of mean-faced men rode out of the aspens. One horse struck a rock with a forehoof and Eb glanced up in time to see all three draw their guns. Without saying a word, the hardcases gunned down Eb and Max and rode off toward the town of Sweetwater, some five miles away.

Fall turned Tombstone, Arizona Territory, golden. The leaves of the few deciduous trees blazed a riot of colors, while the southering sun cast long, yellow rays on the countryside. Residents of the bustling city breathed relieved sighs and went about a great deal more than during the blast-furnace of summer. Fredericksburg Lager Beer—the old Golden Eagle Brewery—opened again, assured now that their fermenting batches would not be spoiled by too much heat. They would continue to turn out a high-quality product, for local consumption, until late April. Drummers began to arrive, to make calls on their customers, hawking everything from apothecary supplies to whiskey. All this quickening of life meant nothing to the couple artfully and amorously engaged in the big bed at the Russ House.

Charity Rose thrashed her head from side to side in a wild spill of her auburn locks, as her moans and sharp cries of ecstasy grew in force and frequency. Her weight supported on her shoulders, buttocks hiked high by four large pillows, she shivered in delight as her passionate lover, Jeremy Ortiz, drove his pulsing member deep within her with each powerful stroke. Hunched on his knees, he thrust back and forth with the powerful spring of youthful muscles.

"Aaaah, Jerry . . ." she wailed as a monumental climax approached, lingered a moment, then crashed over into oblivion.

"Keep . . . with me . . . Char. Ohh, you're . . . soooo . . . fine."

For long, uncounted minutes, their spectacular joining wore on. A fine sheen of perspiration gave Jeremy's light bronze body a glowing nimbus in what sunlight escaped the blinds to filter into the hotel room. His long, thick organ pumped a steady flow from her warm, slippery passage as he strove into her with all his might. Charity placed her feet flat on the sheets and shoved upward to match him stroke for stroke. Jeremy's head swam and his belly muscles ached from exertion. They had been making love since an hour before sunrise. Now he made only the slightest conscious note of it when a small Ormolu clock chimed ten o'clock.

Time meant nothing to him. He had never in his life enjoyed such exquisite lovemaking. What a prize this Charity Rose was. Slow to be aroused, because of an unfortunate experience early in life, once she reached fever pitch she became a wild, uninhibited creature of Eros. Over the long months of their relationship, they

7

had explored every possible means of sharing pleasure. They had invented, as had couples from time immemorial, means to achieve such sheer delight that every encounter held promise of new heights of erotic frenzy.

Charity, likewise, knew of no more fulfilling joy than she received from the sweet and tender ministrations of Jeremy Ortiz. Her heart pounded at the mere thought of their amorous engagements. She shivered as his lips found one erect nipple and began to worry it with tongue and teeth. The long fingers of one hand found her other breast and began to knead it. With resounding rapture they reached a mutual orgasm, shuddering and moaning as they entered the whirlpool of release.

"We are entirely too good together," Jeremy murmured when reason returned. "It has to be a sin to keep all this marvelous talent for ourselves alone. We should share with others, that they might know true joy."

"*Jerry!*" Charity squealed, scandalized. "You are teasing, aren't you?"

Jeremy produced a rueful grin. "Of course I am. I wouldn't share with anyone what I have with you."

"Nor would I," Charity agreed. "Why should I? You are the best, the absolute very best I have ever known. You thrill me, Jerry. And—and I want to keep that all to myself. I—I think the world and all of you."

"Oh?" Jeremy teased. "Prove it, woman."

"I will," Charity promised, squirming around on the bed until her heart-shaped face and auburn hair swung low over Jeremy's groin.

Her nostrils quivered from the heady musk of his male scent. Heat radiated from his well-exercised appendage and she eagerly encircled it with the fingers of one hand. Slowly she stroked new life into the silken flesh. While it

8

slowly rose, she lowered her head even more until her warm breath brushed the sensitive surface of the ruby tip. Her tongue flicked out, circled the dark red nub, slid lower. Jeremy began to writhe and flex his pelvis. Charity opened wide and took him far into her mouth. Jeremy released a stuttering sigh of happiness. With easy strength he began to rearrange her atop him.

Charity spread her legs and shivered with the pleasure his probing fingers brought her susceptible cleft. His tongue followed and sent a jolt of pure delirium through her. Jeremy worked his way deeper within her leafy portal, probing the hollows and curlicues, lancing into her friction-sore passage. She repaid his diligence with increased suction, which brought on a sensation that his member was being pulled out by the roots.

Despite her weight upon him, Jeremy arched his back in ecstatic appreciation and sucked in a long, tremulous breath. It set her off in a whirl of delicious sensations. Charity kneaded at the fat, full sack at the base of his wondrous shaft, tickled it, caressed it, squeezed until Jeremy cried out in wondering zest. His tongue lapped like a hungry kitten.

Throat working, Charity consumed the entirety of Jeremy's ample phallus, her nose nuzzling in the silky black threads at the base. She remained there for long, tantalizing moments, pulsating her larynx in a manner that drove Jeremy wild. Slowly she began to withdraw, lips tightly encasing the rigid shaft, drawing along the velvet hood to once more reveal his blunt, magenta tip. Then she began to describe spirals down the length of his throbbing organ with her dexterous tongue.

Bit by bit the joyous lovers built a glowing, rosy haze around them. Unmindful of anything but their mutual satiation, they drifted deeper into the cosmos until everything outside themselves faded to nonexistence.

Rich and pungent, the heavy aroma of boiled cabbage, ham hocks and potatoes rose from the big cast-iron dutch oven that steamed on the table. In the near distance a tributary of Sweetwater Creek burbled over age-polished stones. Far to the west, the purple slopes of the Sierra Nevada wore sparkling white mantles of early snow. From close to the table a melon-bellied, bearded man called to his two companions.

"It's ready. Come get it, or I'll throw it out."

The three miners sat down to their midday meal with eager anticipation. Quickly the dishes went around, followed by large hunks of crusty sourdough bread. Squirrels scolded from the nearby trees. A fat, saucy cardinal perched on the end of the table, gimlet eye taking in their manners from one side of its scarlet head, then the other. Satisfied, it spread wings, soared to a limb close at hand, and trilled a sweet opinion of their repast.

"We're going to have to get a blacksmith out here to help install that elevator," one observed.

"Still plenty silver on the first level. What's the rush to sink a shaft and open new tunnels?" inquired the youngest.

"There's more down below. You can see the way the vein angles. Once we open that up, we can hire us three—four more fellers, make enough to pay them wages and make us rich," the senior responded, then addressed the first man. "You're right, Al, we'll need a blacksmith. Probably have to build a forge for him."

"If we could find one who'd stay full time, do work for

other outfits, we could take a cut of his profit," Al suggested.

"Now that's what I like, a little enterprise."

Their conversation went on in like vein, the trio of hard-rock excavators unaware of the seven men quietly walking their horses through the yellowing aspens. The seven riders neared the camp and ambled into the natural arbor formed by the widespread branches of ancient cedars. Only then did the youthful miner look up and gave a violent start.

"We, ah, didn't hear you coming," he said as he half rose in greeting, a moment before one of the claim-jumpers shot him between the eyes.

Al tumbled his camp stool over backward, hand streaking for the .45 Colt in the scruffy Army holster with the cut-off flap. He cleared leather in time to put a slug into the beefy shoulder of the closest outlaw. With a yell, the other bandits charged the table. The big, flat boom of a Sharps .56 buffalo gun rolled along the creek. It sent a .56-600 slug into the breastbone of a wild-eyed hardcase and cleared him from the saddle.

Working hastily as he dodged behind a tree, the elder miner chambered another round in the Sharps and took hurried aim. A Winchester and two Colts barked. Two showers of chips marked the strike of two bullets, close enough to cause the miner to waste his shot. He looked up, hopelessly, and found himself surrounded. Slowly he started to lower the rifle.

Four slugs tore into his body, impact triggering uncoordinated reactions by stressed muscles. His grisly dance of death ended with a sighing moan and he flopped onto the pine-needle-strewn ground. Al shot twice at the murderous claim-jumpers, missed both times and sought

11

better shelter.

He rounded the big, grayed Sibley tent that had been their home since coming to mineral-rich Sweetwater Creek. Hot lead tore holes through the heavy canvas, barely missing him. Al gulped in his fear and bent low. He released a sob of relief when he reached the thicket of aspen. They couldn't come after him in there with horses. Fear sweat thick on his forehead, Al wormed his way through the closely packed, thin trunks with their peeling white bark. The quaking aspens lived up to their name as the yellowing leaves shivered and shook above him. Their clatter drowned out any sound save his rasping breath and the thud of his heart. Relying on his exceptional sense of direction, Al angled toward the upper southwest corner of the roughly rectangular stand of trees.

Halfway to his goal, Al sank to his knees and cast nervous glances in every direction. Clearly, over the rattle of the leaves, he heard the shouts of the searching killers.

"Don't let him get away," a commanding voice advised.

"Right, boss. Baudine said no witnesses," came a response.

"He didn't come this way," another hardcase called from Al's right.

"Maybe he circled back," came a suggestion from Al's left.

"Couple of you dismount and start into the trees," Harris ordered.

"Sure, boss. Be careful, Hank, he's got a Winchester," a bass rumble cautioned.

Al crept forward, fighting the fear that consumed him.

12

From behind he heard the rustle of footsteps in fallen leaves. Another fifty yards and he'd be at the edge of the aspens. A sharp pain jabbed through the right side of his chest. He felt weak and the oily sweat ran stingingly into his eyes. If he shot at one of them it would give away his position. What could he do?

Worse, Al reasoned, when he got out of here how could he get away? Haunted by the unanswered questions and the sounds of the methodical search all around him, Al kept moving. Every couple of steps, he glanced behind him. Each time he saw nothing but trees. With tentative, uncertain steps, he reached the upper left-hand corner of the grove. Once more he glanced behind himself and stepped out of his concealment.

Al had a reception committee. Two muzzles bored on him. He barely had time to open his mouth to plead for his life when they spouted flame and smoke. Two slugs tore into his flesh. He dropped his rifle and staggered backward, as though seeking shelter in the aspens. Harris—tall, thin, with hollow cheeks, fired again.

The last thing Al saw was the blue-black smudge of Harris's five o'clock shadow.

"Good morning, Mr. Holoburton," the assayer in Sweetwater gushed.

Concho Bill Baudine covered his mouth with one hand to conceal the self-congratulatory grin that spread at the obsequious man's effusive greeting. Tall and powerfully built, with long, curling blond hair that he now wore clubbed at collar length, Baudine presented a handsome appearance. He had done well in picking an alias for this enterprise, he told himself.

13

He had shed his concho-studded cartridge belt and vest and assumed the garb of a gentleman. Gone also was the low-crowned black Stetson with its telltale leather hatband of brightly shining silver conchos. The pearl-gray bowler he sported reminded him of another notorious outlaw, Bitter Creek Jake Tulley, who had been gunned down a few years back. Jake always wore a derby. Sort of a trademark. Now it served notice on all who saw him that here was a man of distinction and wealth.

Concho Bill frowned when he recalled himself to the present. Letting his mind wander was an early symptom of senility. "I have another test batch from the third level, Mr. Crebs. How soon can we get an assay?"

"Late this afternoon, if you like, Mr. Holoburton."

"That'll be fine. I'll come by at four."

Out on the street, Baudine turned toward the stately, three-story structure that held the Tivoli Palace. He had an important meeting with Frenchy Descoines and Wade Granger and with Gerd Meeker, the manager of his profitable, and entirely legitimate, mine, the Lucky Strike.

CHAPTER 2

Once a week, the assay office in Sweetwater, and the bank, made a shipment of silver to Virginia City. Three wagons, with drivers and guards, and an escort of ten mounted men, usually made the thirty-five-mile journey. Indian Summer still held sway over the valley, with crystal-blue skies, tiny, fleecy cloud puffs and a balmy breeze. This week an additional wagon had been added due to an increased output from the Lucky Strike. The small force set out briskly, dust forming around and behind them in a long, brown haze. The wagons moved at a rough five miles an hour. Heavily laden with silver ingots and bags of nuggets, the four conveyances covered ground at a steady pace. Around them rode the well-armed escorts. They had traveled some ten miles quite uneventfully when trouble caught up to them.

Sharp cracks from parted air and meaty smacks from bullet impacts on flesh gave the first alarm. On the hilly slopes at either side of the road, plumes of powder smoke rose in the underbrush. One driver cried out and pitched headfirst under the left side wheels of his wagon.

15

Another went rigid, then flopped backward onto the canvas cover of his load.

"Jeezus, it's a robbery!" one guard shouted. He discharged his shotgun in the general direction of several puffs of smoke.

"Open 'em up!" the chief guard shouted.

Too late. The surviving drivers found their way blocked by armed, masked men on horseback. More riders pushed in behind and trotted from the trees on both sides. The mounted escort unlimbered weapons and sent answering fire toward the outlaws. Two of them died instantly. Then a hail of bandit lead slashed through the defenders.

"Spread out. Go after the ones in front," the leader shouted to his guards.

"Hell, Myron, they got us cold," one escort drawled laconically.

"You givin' up, Jim?" the leader asked icily.

"Not if you say fight, Myron. But it'll be a little like them Texicans at the Alamo."

"We make 'em pay dear, maybe they'll pull back," Myron suggested. Then to the drivers, "Circle the wagons!"

Wheels creaked and overloaded wagon boxes groaned in protest as the threatened vehicles curved onto uneven ground. Myron took a quick look around and discovered he had lost four men. By his count the enemy had at least twenty, maybe twenty-five. Give up were two words his pappy hadn't had in his vocabulary, and Myron had never learned them either. He drew a bead on one of the outlaws blocking the road to Virginia City and squeezed off a round.

A grunt came from the man a moment before he

16

answered with a bullet of his own. It cracked past Myron's left ear and he fired again. This time his target swayed and then fell forward on his horse's neck. The animal whinnied in fright and started forward. The dead weight on its forequarters added to the horse's general panic and the smell of blood drove it wild. A gap developed in the line as another creature squawled and started to crow-hop.

"Pour it on the front," Myron advised the defenders. "We might break out yet."

Fate had another ending in store for the silver shipment that day. From two sides the mounted outlaws swarmed down on the ring of wagons. Over their heads, sharpshooters picked individual targets among the drivers and guards and dispatched them with morbid efficiency. With bloody regularity, the ranks of defenders dwindled.

At one point, by desperate effort, Myron brought enough fire to bear to make the advance slow and falter. Then the bandits on the backtrail charged into an unprotected quadrant of the circle. Two of them leaped from their mounts and made it to the inside of the hastily made barricades. Myron and Jim turned as one and blasted the pair into eternity. A shrill whistle sounded from in front of the forted-up wagons.

Immediately the bandits pulled off. Tense quiet settled on the besieged wagons. "They had enough?" a teamster asked of no one in particular.

"More likely it's a parley about how best to finish us off," Jim suggested.

"Which gives us time to reload and grab a drink of water. Everyone make yourselves ready for another attack. And don't waste shots on unsure targets. We're gonna run short on ammunition before long."

Ten minutes later the outlaws surged toward the wagons like the horde of Genglis Khan. Firing point-blank into the huddled defenders, they swirled over the scant protection of the low buckboards and brought death and destruction in howling frenzy. Not a man among the defenders remained on his feet, or whole, within five minutes.

Blood ran from wounds and men lay still on the ground. Buck Harris walked over the scene of the final stand with a wide, satisfied grin on his rugged, unmasked face. He'd lost four dead, but that hardly mattered. Enough fast guns and dead consciences lolled around Sweetwater to fill his ranks ten times over.

"Holoburton's gonna be mighty proud of this," he observed.

"Yabbut, it's a lot of his silver we're stealing," one not-so-bright bandit remarked.

"So he gets to sell it again, for a double profit, dummy."

Dull brain wrestling with this idea, the outlaw frowned and worried his lips in a circular motion, disturbing the scraggly threads of an unkempt mustache. "Yeah—yeah, I see. He's mighty smart, that Holoburton."

Harris nodded. "Get these wagons lined out on the road and we'll take 'em to the hideout, boys."

Shivering with cold and nervous reaction, Myron awakened with a monstrous hangover. Dizzy, nauseated and weak, he thought himself blind. Then he realized that he had awakened in that period of intense blackness following false dawn. The bullet that had knocked him down and out cold had left a deep, smarting groove in the flesh above his right ear. Slowly, painfully, he recalled the battle. He tried to sit up, and uttered a ragged groan.

From a short distance away, he heard another human sound of misery. Myron came to his knees and forced himself forward. He found Smitty, one of the drivers. A fumbling, sightless search located a canteen. Myron gave Smitty a long swallow, then had one for himself.

"We fooled 'em," Smitty cackled. "I got a hole in m'shoulder, but it ain't nothin'. I seen 'em comin' an' smeared some blood and brains from Harker on the back of my head. How 'bout you?"

Myron wet his lips. "I took a slug along the side of my head, knocked me out. I must have bled a lot and they took me for a goner."

"The wagons is gone, huh?" Smitty asked rhetorically.

"I suppose so. Be light in a little while. We can see how we stand then."

"Them kind of scum, I wouldn't even look for a horse left behind" was Smitty's opinion.

His prediction proved out. With full daylight, Myron searched fruitlessly for any sign of the wagons, horses, or even the weapons of the fallen men. He did locate three more survivors, whose wounds he treated. Then he washed and re-dressed Smitty's wound, and the older man did the same for him. It helped avoid the realization that they were afoot and miles from help. Two of the revived drivers scratched up enough wood for a fire and sufficient jerky strips from the pockets of corpses to make a thick broth, which they shared.

"Could have sure used some coffee with this," Myron observed with a sigh. "We'll have to head back to Sweetwater."

It took little time to determine that the three drivers Myron had treated would not be able to make the journey. One had a bullet through his left thigh, the other two, injuries that prevented much exertion. Myron assured the others that he and Smitty would send help. Stifling a bitter curse, Myron helped his companion to his feet and they started off in the direction of Sweetwater.

For the first two miles, the headache from his bullet crease plagued Myron enough that he remained conscious of little else. Then the blisters that formed inevitably on the feet of a man unaccustomed to walking more than a block or so began to make their presence felt. He and Smitty hobbled on, Myron biting his lower lip to keep from groaning out his misery. By the fourth mile, they rested for longer periods than they walked.

"If I'd been smart," Myron confided to Smitty, "I'd have played a kid an' gone barefoot. Air don't rub no blisters on the sides of your heel."

"He-heee," Smitty cackled in agreement. "I know what you mean. When I was a little tad, ten—twelve or so, the soles of my feet were harder than any boot sole. Why, I could walk on fire an' not feel it."

Myron blinked owlishly at him. "Bullshit."

"Nope. Gospel truth. Found out by accident. Blundered into a banked campfire and didn't know it until the ragged edges of my pants cuffs started smoldering."

"Ummm. Now you mention it, I recollect running through the backyard, over some busted glass and never gettin' cut. Come to that, I'm for shuckin' these boots right now. This-here road is smooth enough, I'd say."

"He'p yourself. I've enough years on you in shoes not to hazard tryin' it," Smitty confided.

Myron pulled off his stovepipes and peeled away his wet socks. He wriggled his toes, then stood. "Time to move on."

For a while, Myron felt every rock and irregularity in the trail. Manfully he controlled his winces and bit back moans, while his stilted hobble grew gradually smoother until he progressed at an even stride. Smitty cursed under his breath and did his best to keep up. After another mile, they encountered transportation of sorts.

"Looks like you fellers are hurtin' in more ways than one," a grizzled prospector concluded when he examined the survivors of the silver robbery.

"That we are," Smitty agreed. Then he provided a colorful account of the robbery.

"We'd be obliged for any assistance you could give us," Myron added.

Studying the situation, the prospector tugged at his shaggy, gray-shot beard. "Reckon you can double up on that pack mule of mine. He's light-loaded anyhow."

"We accept with deep gratitude," Myron declared dryly.

An hour after midday they reached Sweetwater. By mutual agreement, Myron and Smitty headed directly to the police station. His feet badly swollen, Myron found himself unable to pull on his boots. Cheeks still tinted with a bit of pink from the effort, he entered the chief lawman's office barefoot.

Chief Wade Granger glanced up from his desk with an expression of surprise and consternation. "Myron, Smitty, what are you doing here?" he barked.

Myron studied the ceiling a moment, hoping the chief hadn't noticed his unshod feet. Smitty fixed a hard gaze on the bulbous red nose of the ranking lawman. After

21

their ordeal, his anger had returned with renewed energy, so much so that he viewed Granger's questioning glance as a look of suspicion, although he knew that the cause of the chief's expression was a milky substance in one eye.

"The silver shipment was robbed. Hit about fifteen miles out of town yesterday morning. They musta got a hunnert thousand dollars worth. Only five of us survived, with three unable to travel without help," Smitty stated coldly.

"Be damned!" Chief Granger exploded. "Did anyone get a look at the ones done it?"

"Sure did," Smitty snapped. "An' we talked about it when we come to this mornin'. Myron agrees, it was Buck Harris an' his gang. They had an ambush set up and riders to close in from all sides. We didn't have a chance."

"You're sure it was Buck Harris?" Chief Granger asked, eyes narrowing. "Damn, he's been nothin' but a plague on this town since the rush started. I'll get a posse together and we'll go out and look for any sign. Get a couple of buggies out to help the others, too. You're lucky, the both of you. Harris don't often leave any living witnesses."

"I reckon he thought us dead," Myron added to their narrative. "Y' can see how I got hit alongside of the head. Must have bled a lot."

Granger nodded soberly. "Go see the doc. We can talk this over more while the posse's being rounded up. Damn, Mr. Holoburton'll be furious about this. He had a lot of silver on that shipment."

After the hapless Myron and Smitty departed to see the doctor, Wade Granger allowed himself a slow-blooming smile. The door opened to admit his second-in-command,

Sergeant Chet Bleaker. Quickly he filled Bleaker in on what Smitty and Myron had told him. Then he added a cryptic remark.

"I wonder how much the boys really got?"

Three days had passed since the long night of splendid lovemaking. Now Charity Rose found herself with time on her hands. Not that Jeremy's ardor had cooled, or hers; rather, he devoted his energies to an important case. He was defending a youth charged along with four other boys with stagecoach robbery. The other four had evaded capture, riding south toward Mexico, while the unfortunate youngster had been arrested in a local bordello, after being identified by the victims of the holdup. The small, sallow sixteen-year-old clearly could not have done it, as she had flatly informed Jeremy on the first occasion that she had seen the boy.

This unfortunate lad had the size and development of a boy easily four years younger. He professed to be terrified of guns and the sight of blood made him faint and ill. Charity secretly suspected that the youngster's only sins of commission came from his abundantly apparent effeminacy. Still, she felt sorry for him. Jeremy agreed and went forth to defend the boy. Good, Charity decided. Until time for the trial it would allow her to catch up on events outside Tombstone. Seated in the sun-filled bow window of her hotel suite, she thumbed through a collection of newspapers.

The Tombstone *Epitaph* had a banner headline on the recent gold and silver strikes that abounded around Virginia City, Nevada Territory, already famous for its rich mines of ten years past. Charity read the account

23

with casual interest. Then she turned to newspapers from far off, with more lurid banners and worse prose.

From the pages of the Sacramento *Bee*, she gained an insight into the boisterous doings of the miners and prospectors who swarmed up Sweetwater Creek by day and haunted the saloons, road ranches and bordellos of the unimaginatively named community of Sweetwater by night. Another article in the same paper told of the easy pickings for the industrious, the lucky, and the crooked. Sensationalism, she thought regretfully—not truth—sold newspapers.

In the San Francisco *Chronicle* she came upon a plethora of heavy-handed accounts about the violence and murder, claim-jumping and confidence games.

BLOOD FLOWS IN THE GUTTERS

Under the colorful, bold headline, she found a typical yellow journalism concoction that, surprisingly, held her interest.

Every fast gun, bunco-artist and hoyden has charted course for Virginia City and environs. Following one protracted shoot-out, blood literally ran in the gutters of the nearby town of Sweetwater. Two notorious shootists, Bill Luckenbaugh and Nat Minnows, endeavored to reduce the population of Sweetwater by an even two dozen. They made it to Number Eleven before being cut down by shotguns wielded by Chief of Police Wade Granger and four deputies. Their buckshot-riddled bodies, stripped to the waist to reveal the wounds, were displayed on Main Street, strapped to boards.

"There's been too much killing," Chief Granger declared to this reporter. "We decided to make an object lesson out of these desperados."

Murder alone does not account for the tide of violence engulfing the Virginia City area. Claim-jumping rates high on the list of entertainments in and around the Nevada silver capital. Men are killed in cold blood so that their claims may be assumed by others. Six such incidents occurred last week. In the saloons, stews and road ranches, that old favorite, Mickey Finn, is ordered with all the frequency of demon rum and other ardent spirits. The avaricious painted ladies of Stump Town, Sweetwater and Virginia City quickly pluck the last penny from the unconscious patrons who consume their witches' brew. Rumor has it, and this reporter has developed solid information that indicates it to be true, that a mean-spirited individual has organized a fagin gang, employing the talents of homeless waifs, aged from seven to fifteen, to part the unwary from their cash and valuables, loot stores through entrances impossible for adults to negotiate, and provide other services to those afflicted with dark and unmentionable appetites.

With distaste, Charity put the paper aside. Others would find it unpleasant, or revolting. She found it interesting. Before long, Charity reasoned, the criminal element plaguing the silver rush boomtowns would have prices put on their heads. The more decent people, who traditionally moved into such places in the second or third wave of immigrants, would insist upon it. It wouldn't be long, either, until her resources dwindled to less than two thousand dollars in her bank. Might be that properly approached, the two conditions could nullify each other. She was to meet Jeremy for lunch at the Occidental Saloon at noon. She would put the question to him then.

"You're talking about doing *what?*" Jeremy blurted as they sat at a corner table in the Occidental.

Buckskin Frank Leslie looked up from polishing beer schooners and cocked his head quizzically. He grinned and waggled his mustache, then returned to his labors. Charity frowned, tiny furrows deepening on her brow.

"I've been living the good life too long, Jeremy," she began her prepared argument. "Money's draining out of my account like water from a sprung barrel. I need to go where there's money to be made. Virginia City sounds like the right place. It won't be long before . . ." and she launched into her observations about wanted posters being a part of the civilizing process due any minute to begin in Virginia City.

For his part, Jeremy Ortiz listened patiently to her presentation. He smiled, nodded, murmured at the appropriate places, then spoke his mind. "No. I can't have you wandering off, risking your life, or at the least, disfigurement, while I sit at home playing lawyer."

"But, Jeremy . . ."

"No, and that's that. I'll not hear any more of it. I'm a man who is tired of reading torts and looking up points at law. Right now I want nothing more than to go home, get in bed, and . . . make wild, passionate love all night long."

"Ummmmmm," Charity cooed. "You do know how to

get to a woman's heart."

Rising, Jeremy put a conclusion to any discussion about bounty hunting in Virginia City. "Then that's what we shall do," he said decisively.

They left the opulent dining establishment and walked the dark, quiet streets of Tombstone to Jeremy's small house. They stood admiring the frosty display of stars for several minutes, then went inside and did just that.

CHAPTER 3

Had Charity Rose known that Concho Bill Baudine was included among those profiting illegally from the silver mines and gold fields, she would never have allowed herself to be so easily talked out of leaving immediately for Virginia City. He now operated a somewhat smaller, though considerably more sophisticated, gang. Although prone to violence in order to get their way, Baudine's henchmen also aspired to other talents besides gun-slinging. Quite a few worked in one of the two legitimate fronts Baudine had established, the Tivoli Palace.

The Tivoli was managed by Baudine's partner, Frenchy Descoines. The games were crooked, the whores greedy and prone to roll lower-class customers, and the whiskey incredibly cheap, produced by one of the illegal Baudine enterprises, the Sweetwater Medicinal Herb Company, front for his distillery. Of course, the "quality" patrons received far different service. Like the Tivoli Palace, Baudine's mine was more or less on the up-and-up. Gerd Meeker managed the Lucky Strike. Except for the guards, the employees were regular miners, willing to work for wages instead of striking out on their own to prospect.

While Charity and Jeremy lay naked in each other's arms, Frenchy and Meeker met with Concho Bill to discuss the varied enterprises and the enormous profits. They occupied a comfortable room in the suite of offices rented by "Mr. Holoburton," on the second floor of Sweetwater's only other multistory building. With a light laugh, Frenchy concluded his report on revenue from the Tivoli Palace. "I tell you, Bill, we could give up all the illegal things and still get filthy rich on the income from the Tivoli."

Baudine accepted the truth of his friend's assessment, yet he frowned and framed an answer, for it didn't jibe with his ambition. "No, my friend. Not by half. There's no such thing as having too much money. There's only the agony of not having enough. You have to think big, *mon cher* Maurice—live large."

Maurice Descoines had not seen his childhood friend in such a jovial, expansive mood in years. It encouraged him. "But why spread ourselves so—ah—thin, *mon ami?*"

"I'll repeat myself. Think big. Look at this territory. Outside of the Mormons to the east of us, and this cluster of people around Virginia City, it's a big, open, empty land. You and I, partner, are on the way to becoming millionaires. We can have this land for pennies an acre. One day this will become a state, and you and I will own it all. *That's* what I am dreaming."

"Then you'll be pleased at the contribution of the Lucky Strike," Gerd Meeker inserted. "Fifteen thousand dollars in bar silver in the past two weeks."

"Of course there was that thirty-five thousand we lost

in the robbery," Concho Bill reminded him with a grin.

"Which we will be able to resell for a tidy extra profit," Meeker assured him.

Frenchy Descoines produced a narrow-eyed, doubtful expression. "Aren't those ingots numbered and marked with the smelter's seal?"

Meeker blinked as though he had heard a foolish remark. "Of course. And I'm pleased to announce that we've made ingot molds with the exact pattern of the Sweetwater smelter and a numbering device, thanks to that forger friend of yours."

A bow in recognition of the compliment accompanied Frenchy's smile. A brisk knock announced the arrival of Buck Harris, who entered without pausing.

"Everything we got is safely stowed away. We made all of eighty thousand worth."

"Good work, Buck. The smelter and assay office are claiming over a hundred thousand lost."

Buck Harris grinned. "They would. The load is insured, of course. This way the managers get to line their pockets while protecting their companies' interests. When do we dispose of what we got?"

"See Gerd about when to begin puddling the silver. Once the ingots are cast and cooled, we will have to crate them and ship to Sacramento to dispose of them. Our numbers won't be in sequence," Bill advised. "Now, I want you to send for Wade Granger, Buck. I have a few things to tell him."

"I have a feeling he won't like what you have to say," Buck prompted.

"No, he won't," Concho Bill replied with a mischievous grin.

*   *   *

"Oh, your honor, I must object," Jeremy Ortiz declared dramatically. "This entire disputation is hearsay, assumes facts not in evidence and has no bearing on the case against my client."

"Well, young man," replied the judge, who had no more knowledge of the law than the sixteen-year-old defendant, "I tend to like to hear everything relating to any matter before this court."

Jeremy affected an expression of astonishment. "But this is hardly more than backyard fence gossip!"

"Nevertheless, I think the jury and I would like to hear this," said the judge; then he licked his lips salaciously. "Overruled. Go on."

"Exception, your honor," Jeremy snapped.

In his ignorance of the law and legal terms, Judge Joseph Nicholson eyed Jeremy Ortiz narrowly. "You callin' me out, youngster?"

Jeremy paled. He'd not dreamed of such an interpretation. "No. Of course not, your honor. I merely wanted it in the record that I made exception to your ruling. It's for the appeal."

"I see. Very well. Exception noted. Now, Mr. Prosecutor, will you get on with it?"

"Mrs. Hunter, you say that you heard from your neighbor that the defendant, this 'callow youth' as the defense styles him, had been partaking of the favors of the soiled doves at Miss Tilly's parlor house?"

"Yes," a prim-faced, skinny woman with mousy gray hair answered.

"That, ah, could get to be rather costly, couldn't it?"

"I'm not expert on those things, but I'd say so. No doubt the reason he joined in on that robbery."

"Objection, your honor! I must object most strenuously. The question calls for a conclusion on the part of the witness and the witness made answer on a subject—the state of the defendant's mind—about which she could not possibly have knowledge."

Pulling a long, amused face, Judge Nicholson responded, "Now Counselor, you're a man of the world, of sorts, I'm sure. And I imagine you know that when a young feller gets his pecker up—ah, pardon me, ma'am," he directed to the shocked witness. "When that is the situation, a feller don't often act with intelligence."

"It is still irrelevant, incompetent and inadmissible. Move that this witness's entire testimony be stricken from the record."

"Motion denied."

Jeremy stared at the judge unbelievingly. Ten minutes later court adjourned for the noon hour. Charity Rose joined Jeremy Ortiz in the vestibule of the courthouse.

"This is going to be one hell of a trial," Jeremy remarked, then explained the importance of what had happened that morning.

"Is the judge being paid to insure a conviction?" Charity asked.

"Nooo," Jeremy answered cautiously. "I don't think he's consciously trying to throw the case to the prosecutor. What I do know is that Joe Nicholson is the stupidest judge ever to ride this circuit—or any other, for that matter. I believe Jimmy. He didn't take part in that stage robbery. I'm going to have one hell of a time convincing the jury of that. They'll judge him on his trips to Miss Tilly's and vote for conviction, even if they don't believe he was in on the robbery."

"But that isn't fair," Charity protested.

"Of course it isn't. But it is a clever trick prosecutors frequently employ to insure a conviction. Especially if they have a weak case, like this is. The more checkered a person's past, and the more of it the prosecution can get before a jury, the surer it is that those twelve men, firm and true, will decide that the defendant deserves some sort of punishment."

"And there's nothing you can do?"

"I can find the other four members of the holdup gang and force a confession out of them."

Charity brightened. "No. *I* can do that." At Jeremy's dubious glance she hurried on. "I *am* a bounty hunter, aren't I?"

"Yes, and I've had ample opportunity to verify that," Jeremy allowed ruefully.

"Then I had better get started. It seems to me there is only one place where the robbers could have met Jimmy and through which they could have arranged to set him up to take the blame. I'm going to visit Miss Tilly's."

Conrad O'Farrel had mined coal in Pennsylvania, gold in Colorado, and now silver in Sweetwater, Utah Territory. The rolling Nevada hills had beckoned to him from far-off Cripple Creek. He found work readily available and the pay not too bad, but he still had a large grievance against the Lucky Strike mine.

For all the big pay and relative freedom of a territory rather than a state, Conrad O'Farrel found working conditions abominable. The men were treated like dogs, driven by foremen more concerned with production than safety. With his long experience, Conrad had no difficulty being appointed a shift supervisor, sort of a junior foreman. From then on, he had silently taken the abuse for what the mine boss called slackness on his shift.

He had taken all he could, as a matter of fact. What they needed at the Lucky Strike—at all the mines—was a union. He knew of several lads who had been in the Molly McGuires. Perhaps he should send for one or two of them? Ah, well, so long as he had a full belly, a bucket of beer at the end of shift and someone to warm his bed, why worry?

Conrad started out for his shift with the two questions warring in his mind. The shrilling of the mine's steam whistle put him in a run. At the tunnel entrance, in a billow of dust, twenty men clustered around. Conrad O'Farrel hastened to the spot and thrust several aside.

"What is it?" he asked, only too certain of the answer. "What's gone on?"

"The tunnel shield collapsed over where they're sinking the shaft," a dirty-faced miner told him. "Half the shift's trapped beyond it. Three men got caught in it. They're mashed to red jam."

"Get back there," the mine boss shouted as he approached. "Get some order to you. Second shift, you'll start at once. Get in there and dig out those trapped by the fall."

"We'll have to rig a pipe and bellows first," Conrad stated. "Get air to them, or they'll suffocate."

"Hell with that," the shift foreman growled. "We've got to get it cleared so we can keep the ore moving."

His callous remark decided Conrad O'Farrel. He'd write Sean O'Day right after his shift ended. By God, a good strike might smarten up these brutes.

When C. M. Rose entered Miss Tilly's Recreation Parlor, it set the girls all atwitter. The handsome, almost feminine features of the new patron excited their interest. Many harbored fantasies of the joys to be had in initiating adventuresome young lads into the rites of Eros. The older and more experienced painted ladies knew this to be one of the less pleasurable duties of their calling.

Most often first-timers were nervous, unsure, and utterly ignorant of the mechanics of the required performance. Easily excited, they frequently managed a discharge before effecting any significant penetration. One cynical veteran of twenty-four recalled a lad of tender years, brought by his father to "make a man of him." The poor boy had deposited a warm puddle in her hand the moment she touched his rigid member. He'd spent the next fifteen minutes in a fit of tears from shame and embarrassment. She had been required, she remembered, to do much more than she had been paid for to restore his self-confidence. For all of it, she, too, turned on the charm for the new visitor.

"A friend of mine recommended a certain girl," C. M. informed them.

Their trilling resolved into questions of who that might be. C. M. appeared to be suddenly struck dumb, mouth open, but no name forthcoming. A head shake preceded the next words. "That's funny. I have it on the tip of my tongue . . . but I can't remember. His name is Jimmy Reed."

Several disappointed "Ohs" went the rounds. Then the madam, Tilly, pushed forward a girl C. M. estimated to be no more than fifteen, who looked at least two years younger. "This is Yvette," she said simply.

"Jimmy said you were really great," C. M. declared. Taking her by the elbow, C. M. steered Yvette toward the staircase.

Up in her low, narrow room, C. M. made clear the purpose of the visit. "Jimmy's in trouble."

"I know."

"His attorney doesn't believe he robbed that stage."

"He didn't. He was here when it happened."

Charity frowned at Yvette's statement. Considering the attitude of the judge, she was willing to bet that such a statement, coming from a soiled dove, would be laughed out of court. Perhaps C. M. could get something to provide a more positive showing in front of a jury.

"Do you know if Jimmy was friendly with any other, ah, customers of this place?"

Yvette thought a moment. "Oh, sure. The Grogan brothers and Little Pete Dawkins." She giggled. "It's funny. Little Pete looks enough like Jimmy to be his twin. That's how they met. Little Pete's sweet on Mimi and one night, the first time Jimmy came in, Mimi mistook him for Pete. She had him halfway up the stairs when Pete came storming in. They almost had a fight; then Little Pete realized how the mistake had happened and he started laughing. He and Jimmy became friends and Jimmy got sweet on me that night. Later Little Pete introduced Jimmy to the Grogans. I—don't like them much."

Charity heard little of what Yvette said. She had found what she came for, her hunch node buzzing excitedly in her brain. This could be the connection. No, it *was*, she assured herself.

"Have any of them been in lately?"

Yvette furrowed her brow again. Her rose-bud mouth twisted into a bow. "No, they haven't. Not for some while."

"Like since just after the stage robbery?" Charity prompted.

Light filled Yvette's face and her eyes went wide. "Why, that's it. I never thought of it before, but none of them have been in since that night, and it was only Jimmy."

"Thank you, Yvette. Now, tomorrow, when you're not, ah, working, I want you to go down to Jeremy Ortiz's law office and tell him everything you've told me. I think we can get your Jimmy back for you if you do."

"Oh—oh, really? But, ah, what about now, us? Don't you want to—ah—you know?"

"No, not at all," Charity told her quite truthfully. "I prefer boys."

Yvette made a disgusted face. Charity laughed. "You see, honey, I'm a girl, just like you. Don't tell anyone that, but tell Jeremy that you talked to Charity and she said for you to come in."

"I will," Yvette promised. "You're so cute, I kinda would have liked . . ." She sighed. "But that's out, for sure. Oh, well, I'll save it all for Jimmy."

"Oh, I'm sure you will," Charity replied with only a light touch of cynicism.

CHAPTER 4

Crickets chirped along the creek bank and the desert's night hunters had come out by the time Charity Rose headed her big black gelding, Lucifer, out of Tombstone. She had asked around several saloons for information on the Grogan brothers and Little Pete Dawkins. In the end she had gone to Buckskin Frank Leslie at the Occidental Saloon.

"What's your interest in that collection of mothers' mistakes?" Frank boomed from behind his bar. Charity explained and Frank elaborated on his initial condemnation.

"The Grogan brothers were raised by their mother. The father ran out not long after the last of the pair was born. She had nine other kids and was pregnant at the time he abandoned the family. Howie, who's five years older than his brother, and Frank grew up hell-raisers from the start. Frank's eighteen now, a big strapping hulk of a half-man, with the build of a blacksmith. They walked off and left their mother two years ago, just like the old man. Got it in mind to build themselves a

38

reputation. Not the kind you'd brag about at prayer meetin', either."

"Think they could work themselves up to pulling a stage robbery?" Charity inquired.

Frank twirled the long, waxed ends of his drooping mustache. "Sure they could. At least since they've been hanging out with Curly Reiner and Garth Delevan."

"What about a kid known as Little Pete Dawkins?"

A growl came from under Frank Leslie's big mustache. "Now there's one to steer clear of. Never been known to do anything wrong, exactly. At least nothing he's been caught at and it proven. Sometimes rides for the Pendleton outfit; mostly he lives off of friends and cadges drinks from strangers in return for tellin' wild tales about the Clantons and Earps. He's older and meaner than he looks, with a wild streak a mile wide. Now him I could see throwing in for a holdup any time. What's the interest?"

"We—Jeremy and I—think Pete and the Grogan brothers were in on that stage holdup and Jimmy Reed is innocent. So I'm looking into it. When they're not around town, where do they hang out?"

Frank pursed his lips. "Heard Little Pete mention a two-bit road ranch down toward Sonora way, called Trillbys. That's about the best I can do."

"Thanks, Frank," Charity told him as she patted his arm. "You've done a whole lot."

"You be careful now, you hear me? That Reiner and Delevan are a lot of grief waiting to happen. Why, together they even had Doc Holliday talking politely to them. 'N ya know, Doc's not prone to doin' that to less than four or more. You go around them, watch your back as much as your front."

Charity appreciated the advice. Buckskin Frank Leslie was not a timid man. She returned to the hotel and changed into her C. M. Rose clothes again. At the livery she led Lucifer from his stall. Butch, her half-wolf, half-mastiff, trotted at her side as she rode from Tombstone.

A small, yet intensely dark, cloud hid the sun and provided momentary respite from the relentless heat of the desert. Charity had chosen her tan and brown outfit, something that would blend with the countryside if necessary. The chocolate, flat-crowned Andalusian sombrero concealed her auburn locks, and her sea-green eyes twinkled with the anticipation of the sweet, sharp taste of victory. Her brace of Colt Bisleys rode at her waist in elkhide Lawrence leather. The dark maroon of her morocco boots would match many of the rocks in the Skeleton Canyon country to the south of town.

That ancient arroyo had witnessed so much violence in the past twenty years. A series of washes, rather than a single cut, it made ideal land for the activities of outlaws, smugglers and cattle rustlers. Skeleton Canyon had frequently been an attack route for Apaches and Yaquis. Border lines on maps meant nothing to Indians and both tribes freely raided in Mexico and Arizona Territory. Reflecting on that, Charity knew she had one more danger to keep in mind. She knew of Trillbys, by its unsavory reputation, if not from personal experience.

A pair of crumbling adobes—once the home of a Mexican family—with a pole-frame, palmetto leaf thatch palapa forming a causeway between them, the road ranch had pounded dirt floors, dug two feet below ground level. There was a corral of sorts, with a rudimentary shade for horses, a well, and a wide, glittering yard of smashed bottles, thrown out after being emptied, surrounded it. Reputed to be a haven for the territory's hardcases,

40

Trillbys did a profitable business, despite its remote location. Charity decided to give it a wide sweep and size up who and how many customers might occupy the notorious saloon.

What she learned would determine her plan of approach. It might be she could ride straight in and catch the men she sought sodden with booze. In that case, it would all be over in an afternoon. The sun came out from behind the small cloud and Charity began to perspire. Rivulets of salt moisture ran down her back and from under her arms. As the miles wore on, she began to long for any body of water, and its cooling refreshment. Her mouth grew cottony and she fetched a small pebble from a vest pocket and popped it under her tongue.

In a moment moisture began to flow and her demanding thirst diminished. Another twenty miles at least, she calculated. How she would love to throw herself into the soothing waters of Padre Tanks, close to her home of Dos Cabezas. Thoughts of the tanks summoned other images.

Thirteen-year-old Charity Rose and white-haired Corey Willis, the same age, naked bodies sparkling and slick with the water they had climbed from. They embraced, kissed, and Charity thrilled to the demanding pressure of Corey's rigid member, pressed against her lower belly. Tom Thornton, tall, lean, so manly, such a magnificent lover. She shared the enchantment of the tanks with him, also. Both gone now; Corey moved away two years after they discovered love together, Tom tragically in his grave. With determined effort, Charity forced her memories beneath the surface and concentrated on the too-real hazards around her.

*   *   *

Della Terrace adjusted the big, red feather that rose from the right side of her waist in a huge question mark that encircled her left breast. The black net dress she wore, with hem at mid-thigh, cunningly accented her scarlet and ebon underthings. Her long, shapely legs were encased in stockings of crimson silk net. She gave her attire and endowments a critical examination in the full-length, oval, bevel-edged mirror in its walnut stand. Nodding her satisfaction, she left her room for the large common room downstairs in the Tivoli Palace.

"You're lovely tonight, dear," Mattie Orcutt purred as she placed a pudgy, beringed hand on Della's shoulder.

Della cringed away. She disliked other women touching her. But this was the boss and she had to put a good face on it. "Thank you, Mattie. I hope my first night here will be as profitable as you said."

"In that get-up you'll knock 'em dead, kid," Mattie replied, a bawdy tone coloring her words.

"I'd prefer them alive, and hungry," Della quipped.

"Oh, my dear, you could give a dead man a stiff pecker," Mattie cooed.

Coarse langauge also offended Della, though she affected not to show it. She eased her way past the madam and walked the hall to the stairway. The only three-story building so far completed in Sweetwater, the Tivoli Palace managed every night to fill to capacity its saloons, gambling hall and the cribs of the soiled doves. Della considered herself fortunate to be accepted for employment there. A freelance girl, without boyfriend or madam to look out after her, often found it difficult to know where the next bite of bread might come from. While she descended the curving staircase, through the great open space that extended fully to the skylights above the third floor, she took in the glittering panoply below.

Waiters in white gloves and jackets and black-striped trousers moved among the tables and the standing patrons with drinks, boxes of cigars and canapes on silver trays. In sharp contrast, most of the customers wore the rough clothing of miners and prospectors. Only here and there did she see a suitcoat, and only one set of formal attire. That would be Frenchy Descoines, the over-all manager.

Frenchy had interviewed her, as well as Mattie. He had asked probing questions about any family, whether she supported a procurer, whether she had children. Not once did he show the least turn of interest in her. She might as well be a slab of beef. Della didn't flatter herself with false modesty. She firmly believed that any male from twelve to eighty who didn't get a rise out of looking at her was either impotent or a sissy. But then, when Frenchy had come to her room to claim his *droit de maison,* she found him possessed of a frenzied and almost insatiable sexual energy.

Yet he remained so outwardly cool in front of others. Almost like a hardened killer. The thought gave her a shiver as she cleared the last treads and stepped into the festive throng. Tonight she would start earning her keep. And who knew? She might find a rich prospector and live happily ever after.

C. M. Rose had waited until well after nightfall. A count of horses in the corral revealed a potential of eleven men inside, not counting the proprietor-bartender, the bouncer, and three slatternly whores. Through the dregs of late afternoon, three men in the

Charro costumes of Mexican vaqueros got boisterously drunk at one table under the palapa. Four hardcases with the pallid skin and nervous glances of recently released— or escaped—convicts occupied another corner and drank in sullen silence. That left a quartet unaccounted for inside the saloon.

While the waning sun cast bars of magenta, crimson and silver from behind distant Hereford and Miller peaks, a slightly built young man trotted his horse to the corral and dismounted. He matched the description given of Little Pete Dawkins. That gave Charity a fair idea of who might be in the bar. Still she held her peace. Time and more liquor would work their attrition on the number of guns she might have to face. The four jailbirds rode out around ten o'clock. Still she kept to the outer blackness, some fifty yards now from the road ranch.

Her moment came when one of the vaqueros staggered out into the darkness and vomited. Then he wove his way back to the table to slump his head in his arms and snore softly like his companions. C. M. Rose, with Butch alongside, rose and headed for Trillbys. Colt Bisley in hand, the bounty hunter closed on the shaded patio.

Blurred forms came into sharp resolution and a fat desert rattler buzzed indignantly off to one side. Sotted to the point of unconsciousness, the vaqueros snored away as C. M. Rose passed them by. The two adobe buildings loomed ahead, to the right the sleeping quarters for employees and guests, on the left the saloon. A single dim kerosene lantern illuminated the interior.

"Gotta piss," a voice broke the eerie silence.

C. M. Rose checked as a dark figure blotted out the yellow glow of lamplight. A burly man, who must have been Garth Delevan, wove his way onto the patio. He

44

didn't bother with even the rudiments of sanitation. Opening his fly, he withdrew his penis and urinated on the flagstones of the breezeway. Delevan had just grunted his relief and squeezed off the last drop when C. M. Rose slipped up beside him and clouted him on the temple with the heavy, thick barrel of a Colt Bisley.

Delevan went to his knees, reached vaguely for his agonized head and dropped face first in the spreading pool of his waste. C. M. Rose stepped fastidiously over the puddle and entered the doorway, Bisley cocked and ready. Four men looked up from a shabby green baize table.

"What—? Where's Garth?" one of the Grogan brothers slurred.

"He's sleeping. All four of you place your hands on the top of the table. Move slowly or I'll put a hole through you," C. M. Rose demanded.

"Who the hell are you?"

"What do you think you're doing?"

Charity, as C. M., answered both questions. She concluded with, "I'm going to get some answers out of you here, or in the jail at Tombstone."

"There's only one of you," Little Pete sneered.

"And only four of you. Which leaves two bullets for the bartender if he doesn't take his hand away from the gun under the bar," C. M. added in a raised voice.

Under his olive complexion, the Mexican barkeep paled and froze where he stood, with one hand under the bar. C. M. nodded at him.

"Take your hand out slowly."

When he complied, Curly Reiner pushed his luck. His .44 Remington cleared leather and came nearly above the level of the table before C. M. Rose shot him between the eyes. He flopped backward, overturning his chair, and lay sprawled on the dirt floor. Blood soaked thirstily into the ground. Little Pete pushed back from his place and dipped a hand to his sixgun. A blur flashed across the vision of everyone in the room and Little Pete found himself with his wrist tightly clamped in the jaws of a snarling, gray-black beast.

"Yaowww! Lemme go, lemme go!" Little Pete Dawkins howled in a thin, soprano voice as the sharp, white teeth punctured skin and sank into flesh.

"Butch, *amach,*" C. M. commanded as Pete's sixgun thudded to the tamped floor.

Butch released his victim and took two wary steps backward. His gold wolf's eyes remained fixed on the short outlaw. Little Pete clasped his injured wrist with the other hand and bent over, sobbing in agony.

"Goddamn you," he gulped, then shrieked, "*Goddamn you!* You ruint my gunhand."

"I understand you won't be needing it on the gallows," C. M. told him coldly.

Helplessly, the Grogan brothers fumed at their surprising capture. Frank, the younger, asked a whining question. "What are you doing this for?"

"I'll say it again. You're wanted for that stage robbery you pulled off last month. I'm taking you in to Tombstone."

"We didn' do nothin'," Frank bleated. "That was that funny kid looks like Little Petey."

"Jimmy Reed?" C. M. asked.

"Yeah. That's the one. Funny how he looks so much like Li'l Pete."

"Enough so that frightened stage passengers, at night, would mistake one for the other?" C. M. prompted.

"Sure. That's how Gerd and Howie had it figured. It wor—"

"Shut up, you half-wit!" Howie Grogan screamed at his brother.

"Goddamn idjit," Little Pete snarled.

"On the floor, all of you. On your bellies," C. M. commanded, producing cuffs from a pocket of the canvas coat. "Stretch your hands out."

"I can't," Little Pete complained. "That mangy cur of yours near bit one of mine off."

"I'll put him to work on your neck if you don't do what I say," came a cold warning.

"All right—all right," Little Pete whined.

"That's fine, boys. By noon tomorrow, you'll all be nice and comfortable in the Tombstone jail."

CHAPTER 5

Gnats swarmed in a thick cloud near her face. Charity
Rose lay on the sandy soil, protected by the rise of a ridge
in front, burned by the sun above. With a suddenness
that allowed no preparation, she had found herself
harassed by half a dozen border ruffians, summoned to
rescue their comrades. The Grogan brothers, Garth
Delevan and Little Pete Dawkins now lay lower down the
ridge, legs chained around a saguaro cactus. Charity, still
in her garb as C. M. Rose, had made it nearly to Ike
Clanton's ranch headquarters when the avenging hooli-
gans had caught up. Leading her prisoners' horses, she
sprinted over a low hummock of sand and along a side
draw until she reached the present position. There had
been eight of them to begin with.

Two tasted of her accuracy with a Winchester and lay
sprawled on the desert floor. The remaining six had
drawn off to discuss strategy. They needn't have a great
deal of it, Charity considered. All it required was for some
of them to ride around one way or another and come at
her from behind. No matter what direction she turned,

her back would always be vulnerable. She wet her lips and selected a pebble from the ground to suck on.

Thirty feet separated her from her canteen and she had no desire to move as yet. A little whiff of dust, rising from an adjacent arroyo, informed her of when the bandits had discovered the obvious. That would be two, perhaps three men. Charity fought the tension that threatened to render her motionless. She had to keep her head about her. How long did she have left?

Dull thuds from a flurry of hoofbeats brought her attention to the front. Two men, bent low over the necks of their mounts, raced toward her. When the range closed sufficiently, they fired sixguns in a wide swath along the crest of the ridge. Charity sighted on one and fired, rolled twice and came to her knee to trigger another round.

A horse squealed pitifully while Charity rolled to another position. She came up in time to see the mortally wounded animal break stride and lunge forward, casting its rider free to tumble head over heels across the sand. Before she could take another position, the remaining attacker swerved away, did a running pick-up of his companion, and they pelted back to the safety of a cluster of rocks. Her hat had flown from her head and the wind blew long strands of her auburn locks across her face. She brushed at them with an unconscious motion. Suddenly Charity realized she had momentarily forgotten about the outlaws circling to hit her from behind.

The loud crash of gunfire to her rear brought her around, swinging up the Winchester far too late. A scruffy individual wearing three coats, fingerless gloves and a food-soiled vest staggered into view, bleeding from two wounds in his chest. From the opposite direction, the other gunmen renewed their attack.

Charity spared only a moment to watch the wounded outlaw fall dead, then gave her attention to his friends. She cycled three more rounds through the Winchester, then paused to thumb fresh cartridges into the loading gate.

"You're gonna die out here," Pete Dawkins taunted her. "My friends are goin' to finish you off."

"You won't be around to celebrate," Charity told him coldly. "Before they get me I'll kill every one of you."

Charity turned back to the fight, ignoring them. She could see the muzzle-bloom of the attackers' Colts when she shouldered the Winchester again. Her first shot cleared a man from the saddle, a nasty wound in his belly. The second cut through the ear of a horse and spanged off the saddle horn. Cursing, the rider swerved away and headed for points south. Loyalty to a brother outlaw went only so far when facing such deadly accuracy. Only the wounded and dead remained behind.

Hunched and tensed for action, Charity waited a good ten minutes before she lowered her rifle and stumbled to the canteen. Although tepid, the water tasted heavenly as she took a good, long swallow. A tingling glow of almost sensual pleasure washed through her. Then the reaction to fighting and killing took hold.

Coughing and gagging, Charity bent double, arms hugging her belly. She didn't vomit; her past years of experience in the violent, bloody occupation she had chosen had inured her enough for that. Still, the emotional effect of danger, of taking a human life, and the closeness of her own death tore at her inner being. Her mouth tasted of oiled brass, her eyes burned and stung, her throat cramped and ached, and she wanted desperately and immediately to make furious, passionate love. God, how she hurt.

"Ooo-wiee! Shouldn't a nice girl like you be mixing it up with border scum like them," a voice reached her. She yanked her head and her Bisley up together.

"Whoa, now. I ain't gonna make you no trouble. Never knowed it was a girl when I saw them fellers makin' to bushwhack you. Thought you could use a hand. M'name's Billy, Billy Clanton."

Charity's eyes widened. "Billy. I'm Charity Rose."

"Pleasure. What're you doin' with those fellers chained up like that?"

"I'm taking them in to Tombstone for that stage robbery last month," Charity told him simply, wondering what this notorious rustler and sometime gunfighter would make of that.

Billy Clanton beamed like a kid with a new toy. "Good on you. The new sheriff tried to pin that on me an' some friends. But I heard they caught one of them. A boy name of Jimmy . . ."

"Reed," Charity completed. "He didn't do it, and I made up my mind to find the ones who did."

Billy surveyed the carnage. He'd nicked one, killed another. She had four finished off to her credit. He let go a low whistle. "Damn—ah, pardon, Miss Charity—sure looks like you knew what you were doing. Where'd you take 'em?"

"At Trillbys," Charity stated simply, reaction to the violence still plaguing her.

Billy gulped and whistled again. "You have any help?"

"My dog."

Butch's head came up and Billy surveyed the display of long, white teeth. "Lord A'Mighty, looks like you didn't

51

need much more than that. Would ya—would you like some company on the way in to town?"

Charity searched her jangled emotions and came up with a brief smile. "Why not? I'd like that, Billy."

"I'll fetch my horse."

When they reached the streets of Tombstone and people began to gather on the boardwalks to gawk, Billy leaned close to Charity and spoke in a whisper. "Half the folks in this town think I'm a bas—ah—bad man, and the other half think I'm a poor, innocent victim of the Earps."

Charity had recovered her aplomb, along with her C. M. Rose persona, and replied teasingly, "Which one is the truth, Billy?" His jaw dropped and then worked wildly as he tried to frame an answer. "Don't bother to reply," Charity added hastily.

At the jail, Charity turned over her prisoners and Billy Clanton declared loudly to the gathered crowd, "I di'n't have nothin' to do with it. I just rode in with—ah—C. M. here from our spread. Seems some folks took offense at him bringing in their pals. I'll see you again—ah—C. M."

"I hope so, Billy," Charity said brightly as the young sometime outlaw pushed through the throng of citizens.

Jeremy came rushing up, informed of her arrival. "Was that Billy Clanton?"

"Why, yes, it was, Jeremy," Charity answered. "He seems like a nice boy."

"He's a snake," Jeremy said hotly.

"He saved my fanny out there on the desert," she defended stoutly.

"He—ah—well . . . perhaps . . . Do you have any good news for me?" Jeremy changed the subject.

"I do. Inside the jail. I caught the whole gang responsible for that robbery."

"Good. Now if I can get that moronic judge to listen to the truth," Jeremy speculated.

"Yes, but after I get cleaned up, have something to eat and we get a good night's rest."

Looking ill-at-ease, Jeremy guided Charity off to one side. "If you take to saying things like that, C. M., people are going to start to talk. Remember who you are."

Charity gave a quick glance to her man's clothing and began to giggle, a reaction left over from the hours of danger she had endured. "When I get out of these clothes, there'll be no doubt of how I intend to spend the night."

Word had gone around Tombstone at lightning speed. Early the next morning, spectators spilled out onto the steps of the Cochise County Courthouse, and spread on the lawn. Resident deputy sheriff, Billy King, along with three deputies, had all they could do to maintain order. Hawkers went about selling wiener sausages (hot dogs), iced bottles of Fredericksburg Lager Beer from the former Eagle Brewery, boater straw hats for the gentlemen, and lemonade. The Tombstone *Nugget* had taken a clear stand for "law and order," in typical disregard for accuracy and facts, with a scathing editorial about "shiftless" defense attorneys who "manufactured" evidence to free their clients.

The opposition Republican newspaper, the *Epitaph,* lauded the courage of the young bounty hunter, who, in the glowing words of the editor and town mayor, John P. Clum, had single-handedly rounded up the real culprits. Tension reached a palpable presence when defense attorney Jeremy Ortiz rose to address the bench.

"At this time, your honor, I would like to introduce a motion for dismissal of all charges against my client."

"Motion denied," Judge Nicholson snapped automatically.

"Then I call as my first witness, Peter Dawkins. Since he is presently residing in jail," Jeremy said drolly, "it will take a few minutes for Sheriff King to bring him here. While we're waiting, I would like to lay a little groundwork." Billy King departed for the jail in the cellar, while Jeremy continued.

"Cases of mistaken identity are not uncommon," he began. "People of Arizona Territory *vs* Stoddard, Appellant Proceedings at two thirty-five. Also People of Kansas *vs* Hanson, Jennings et al, Kansas Appellant One at five-oh-two. I have a dozen other citations," Jeremy added, "but they are in my brief of the motion, and I'll not bore the bench or the jury with reciting them now. Suffice to say that under the stress of an act of violence, and particularly at night, persons can easily become confused. And particularly so again, if the accused and another person bear a remarkably close similarity in appearance."

"What is the point of all this, Mr. Ortiz?" the judge growled.

Jeremy half turned toward the jury, raised his hands before him, palms up, and rolled his eyes heavenward as though in supplication. "To show reasonable doubt, your honor. No—more than that—to achieve an acquittal for my client. With the evidence recently uncovered, with the entire gang behind bars—at least those not deceased during their capture—and in light of the denial of my motion, I will be satisfied with nothing less than a true bill of acquittal by this jury."

Judge Nicholson had begun a sharp reprimand abut the propriety of such a statement being made out of the presence of the jury when Billy King returned with his prisoner. The murmurs began the moment the pair entered the courtroom and grew in volume as Little Pete and the deputy sheriff advanced to the bar. The jurors exchanged glances with each other and nodded heads. Jeremy produced his most winning smile.

"Your honor, I requested and was granted the reservation to recall prosecution witnesses for further cross-examination. I would like to do so at this time. I call Dan Jenner, Lucy Frank, Milt Banner to the stand at once. I would like them to take a look at this young man, the defendant, and at this one, and tell the court which it was whose bandanna mask fell down in the course of the stage robbery and made his features known to them."

Fourth of July fireworks would have caused less excitement in the courtroom. It took a full minute of violent rapping of his gavel for Judge Nicholson to restore order. He glowered at the chastened observers and waggled an admonitory finger.

"There will be no further outbursts such as that disgraceful display, or I shall have the sheriff clear the courtroom. Your strategy is highly irregular, Counselor."

"I merely wanted to save the court time, rather than parade them one at a time and have them say the same thing," Jeremy responded, managing to sound the offended party despite his elation.

Joseph Nicholson's sagging jowls flamed scarlet and he pinched his nose in a habitual gesture. "Does the People have any objection?"

Aware of the shambles of his case, the prosecutor answered the judge with a shrug, then spoke quietly. "None, your honor."

At the victory celebration thrown by Jimmy Reed's family, Jeremy Ortiz and Charity Rose were the guests of honor. Flushed with the realization of his vindication, Jimmy expressed the sentiments of his family when he lamented that the man responsible, C. M. Rose, had not been located to attend. He commented weakly that at least one member of the Rose clan had come, and urged her to convey his gratitude. He flushed with considerable embarrassment when Jeremy took him aside, swore him to secrecy, and then revealed that the C. M. in the bounty hunter's name stood for Charity Moira.

ORGANIZED BANDITRY BLAMED IN SWEETWATER PERILS

Charity Rose read the bold headline in the Sacramento *Bee* while a crease formed on her clear, high forehead. The story that followed the senationalist caption did nothing to calm her growing unease. Jeremy Ortiz leaned over the upholstered back of the Prince Albert chair and kissed her at the base of her neck. She raised a hand to his cheek in affection while she squirmed away from the momentary distraction.

"You're chafing at the bit," Jeremy remarked tritely.

"Like any good war horse when it smells the odor of battle," Charity played on the line. "Jeremy, there's a lot going on up there that the newspapers aren't telling us. At least not in one reasonable and properly verified story. And, as I've said before, there's money to be made. By now there will be wanted flyers on any number of the outlaws operating around Virginia City. I need to enlarge my bank account and there's no time like the present to do it."

"You mean right now? This minute?" Jeremy blurted.

"Well, I—er, ah, of course not."

"I was in hopes you could come up with a more exciting idea of what we might do right now." Jeremy's hands slid over her creamy shoulders, down to the swell of her firm, pert young breasts.

Charity sighed contentedly. "Oh, I can think of several things," she prompted.

"Such as?"

Disengaging his hands, she rose and faced him. "How about throwing off our clothes and making wild, passionate love right here in front of your fireplace?"

"Ummm—un-uh. I don't like getting rug burns on my knees, and I sure don't want you getting any on your pretty little a—"

"Don't say it!" Charity squeaked, putting two fingers over his lips. Slowly she began to unbutton her dress.

Jeremy swallowed hard and stood back to watch her. It took little time for her fingers to make the journey from neck to waist. She shrugged out of the long sleeves and the entire facade fell forward and then sank around her ankles. Her lovely, mellow breasts stood up proudly. At her waist the pull-string-tied pale yellow chemise covered her lower parts. She quickly divested herself of this and stepped out of her clothes.

A gasp came from Jeremy as he took in her beauty, flickeringly illuminated by the crackling fire on the grate behind him. Charity produced a seductive smile and stepped toward him. Nimbly she unfastened his vest, then undid the buttons of his shirt. She pulled the starched white tails free of his trousers and bared him to the waist. His golden skin seemed to ripple in the firelight.

Coyly, Charity wet a fingertip with her tongue and began to trace circles around the small darker discs of his nipples, thrilling to their instant engorgement and rise. Her imagination filled in a similar event occurring below. Wetting her index finger again, she ran along the slightly indented line at the center of his chest, onto his flat, muscular belly, and ended at the small knot of his navel.

This, too, received a stimulating circular caress. His belt came free in an instant and the buttons of his fly yielded rapidly to her efforts. His trousers dropped around his ankles, revealing the long, fat bulge in his underdrawers. Charity used both hands to encompass his endowments, gently squeezing and sliding up and down. Jeremy's eyes roved over her delightful body, from the sweep of her auburn locks to the severe little V of her nearly hairless pubic mound. She glistened wetly ready in the sudden flare of a resinous piñon log. Jeremy freed himself from his clothing and removed his shoes.

"You're the most beautiful woman I've ever seen," he panted.

"You'll have to do better than that. You've said that a lot of times," Charity teased, fully aroused now and eager to begin their joyful communion.

"You are a whole galaxy of loveliness." It had no effect

on the tiny, affected frown of boredom. "The world would end if your beauty was taken from it." Still no change. His failure at eloquence set him to stammering. "Ah—I—ah—" Suddenly he took Charity in his arms and lowered her toward the floor. "To hell with rug burns. My knees will heal."

"*Now* you've gotten through to me," Charity gusted out.

He entered her forcefully, eagerly, thrusting until he hilted his lengthy manhood and his pubis slammed against her fevered cleft. Charity moaned and wrapped her legs around his waist, locking her ankles at the small of his back and straining to take more than he could give. His breath played across her face, warm and sweet. They kissed and Jeremy began to piston his loins. So aroused had they both become that their best efforts prolonged the inevitable for less than fifteen minutes.

Charity thrashed her head and cried out in the moment of her completion and then lay under his welcome weight, panting and gasping while he slowly, tauntingly worked his member in her burning vise-like grip. At last he withdrew and lay beside her.

"I want it to go on for ever," Jeremy gulped out.

"So do I, dearest," Charity agreed.

"Then you won't leave me, lady?" he said hopefully.

"Not—not for a while. At least not until we manage that much splendor again and again all night long."

"Oh, we will. We will do that," Jeremy assured her, tingling to a resurgence of power in his mighty organ.

"I hope so, Jerry. It will have to last us . . . a while."

CHAPTER 6

Dry, brown, stunted vegetation along the coastal plain gave way to the blue-green richness of pine forest as the Southern Pacific Daylight Express from Los Angeles to Sacramento wound through the foothills of the San Gabriel Mountains, north of the City of Angels, and into the fertile valley beyond. Seated in the Pullman-designed dining car, Charity Rose lunched on fresh oysters, hot-from-the-oven sourdough bread and such exotic fruits as oranges, artichokes and avocado. The journey from Tombstone to Los Angeles had been arduous.

The desert in which she had lived since early childhood extended all the way to the western slopes of the Coastal Range. She had traveled by stage coach to Indio, where the Santa Fe spur line took her to the small inland city, called by the Spanish *Ciudad de Nuestra Señora la Reina de los Angeles*. Charity's familiarity with the language caused her to doubt that Our Lady, the Queen of Angels, had ever smiled benevolently upon such squalor. Boarding the Union Pacific Daylight Express, after securing Lucifer and Butch in the livestock car, restored her outlook for the success of the trip. The ascent into the Los Padres Mountains brought new wonders to behold.

Charity had just returned to her seat in the Pullman sleeper coach when a flat rumble far forward reached the car. Suddenly metal shrilled beneath her feet. The train lurched and began to slow. Curious, she leaned over to peer out the window. While momentum paid off, the cars glided past a line of dark-faced men with ebon eyes and flowing mustaches under huge sombreros. Mounted on an assortment of horses, the riders bristled with weapons and sat in ornate Mexican saddles with large pommels and huge horns. Some sort of performing group on their way to a festival, Charity speculated before she heard the first dull pops of discharging firearms.

"Train robbery!" she announced, somewhat louder than she had expected.

Women screamed and children cried, men bolted from their seats in pandemonium or sat rigid and white-faced. The line of bandits in *Charro* costume rode forward and boarded the train at the ends of each car. Charity stood erect and pulled the latch to release her sleeping berth. When it dropped down it revealed a fair-sized carpetbag, from which she took her Colt Bisleys and the Lawrence rig. A moment later the doors flew open with such violence that the glass panes shattered.

Two bandits entered at both ends. Dressed in a variety of gold-and-silver-embroidered suits of tan, chocolate, black and gray, they swaggered into the center aisle.

"¡Los manos arriba, gringos!" one of them sneered.

A young man at the front of the Pullman shot the bandit closest to Charity and she did the same for him. Startled by such sudden and effective resistance, the

61

other pair froze. Charity's Bisley barked and the second train robber fell on the legs of his partner. The determined-looking young man quickly finished off the last outlaw.

"Some of you grab up their weapons and make yourselves useful," Charity shouted to the stunned passengers. "You're not going to let them rob this train, are you?"

"Look at her," the other defender took up. "She's done in two of them. Surely some of you can do as well."

"It's not our business," a prim, pinched-faced man in an expensive suit rejected. "It's the railroad's job to protect us."

"That's a great attitude," the youthful gunman sneered. "Only right now it don't matter worth a pinch of coon shit."

"Go on, take their guns and let's drive the bandits off the train," Charity urged. "You two, bend down and pick up those sixguns."

Caught in the middle of the aisle, the pair gave Charity rueful grins. "Don't need to. We were goin' for our guns when you two started shooting."

"Good. Go ahead and do it, then pass out the dead men's weapons. That makes four of us," Charity announced to the other passengers. "Haven't any of you fine gentlemen as much courage as a—look out!" Charity's Bisley spoke again and a fierce-faced bandito staggered back out onto the vestibule, to fall in a pool of his own gore.

"Thanks," the young man said through a grin. "I'm Josh Blaine. I've never come across a lady who can shoot so well. Ah—not that I'm complaining," he added hastily.

"Thank you, Mr. Blaine. Charity Rose."

"Josh. Under the circumstances, first names will save time, Charity."

"Agreed."

"You two through passin' the time o' day?" grumbled one of the volunteers. "There's some more of those bandits making to rush this car."

He called himself Joaquin Murrieta. He thought he was around twenty-five years old, with the smooth face of a child, marred by a large, hook nose and a brave attempt at a full, flowing mustache. The real Joaquin Murrieta had been dead, his head pickled in a jar, for more than thirty years. Like his namesake, young Murrieta styled himself a heroic figure, a Robin Hood, fighting for his people's rights against the *gringo* thieves who had stolen California from them. In the plain language of the day, he robbed people.

Trains had replaced stagecoaches in much of California which suited the youthful Joaquin quite well. Trains carried more money, and it was more exciting to rob a train. When it came to robbing from the rich, Joaquin excelled at it. Giving the proceeds to the poor, Joaquin assigned to *mañana* which, as everyone knew, was also another day. He had decided to hold up the Daylight Express because it would be his most ambitious undertaking so far. In his carefully laid plans, he made only one slight miscalculation.

He hadn't counted on any form of resistance from the passengers. The express car crewmen might put up a fight, perhaps even the conductor, but not the over-fed and pampered *gringos* in their fancy clothes. They would grovel and whine and hand over their valuables. Even had he been able to read, and come across a list of those aboard, the name Charity Rose would have meant nothing to Joaquin. Not long after the attack began, he belatedly learned of his error.

"Juan, Ruben, Jorge, *¡subirlos al tren!*" Joaquin shouted when rapid shots came from inside the Pullman car. *"Tenermos mala pena."*

Three of the bandits reluctantly started for the car as ordered. They had clearly heard the sound of the bad trouble Joaquin referred to. Easing their way up the cast-iron steps, they reached the vestibule. Juan quickly saw the difficulty. Several passengers were armed and had already downed the men sent to rob them. Juan took a deep breath and jumped through the doorway.

"Look out!" a feminine voice shouted, the blast of the .45 Bisley in her hand following immediately.

Juan staggered back onto the plates of the platform and fell in a welter of blood. *"¡Dios!"* Ruben exclaimed, crossing himself.

Bent low, goaded by the voice of their leader from outside, Jorge and Ruben dashed into the car. Gunfire seemed to come from every part of the Pullman. Pain and shock flashed, to be numbed by dimming brains. Leaking from half a dozen wounds, Jorge reeled halfway into the car and shot a man in the shoulder before he fell dead. Ruben sought a way out and went off to meet his maker in another rapid-fire burst of hot lead.

Enraged at this obvious, and visible, failure, Joaquin screamed incoherently and bashed his left fist against the fat mushroom of his saddle horn. He put spurs to his mount and moved forward, where events went more according to plan. Two of his men, he saw, had affixed a dynamite charge to the door of the express car. Already the short fuse sputtered and smoked.

"Two of you stay here to hold the car," Charity commanded. "The rest of us will go forward and clear the bandits off the train."

Josh Blaine found himself taking orders from a woman and not resenting it at all. She sure knew what she was doing, handled herself well, and was a hell of a shot. Nor had she gone off into feminine vapors when the bandits had been blasted. Grinning with battle joy, he shouldered his way to her side as they started for the next coach.

Well disciplined, the robbers in the car ignored the sounds of fighting around them to complete their task of stripping passengers of money and valuables. They had nearly reached the midpoint when Charity and Josh burst into the parlor coach. One chubby bandit turned, gape-mouthed, toward them.

"*¿Que es esto?*" he managed before two .45 rounds cut him down.

His companions dived for cover. A woman screamed and fainted. Her husband let out a bellow and clouted a dodging outlaw alongside the head. The outraged man swept up the unconscious robber's sixgun and triggered a round that struck off the heel of another outlaw's boot.

"Keep their heads down," Charity ordered the belligerent passenger. "One of you stay here to help him."

On the next vestibule, Charity found the dead conductor. He had fired his revolver at least once, she noted in passing. In the next chair car the bandits had finished their work and departed. Cowed, though indignant, the passengers blinked stupidly at the armed band of fellows who rushed along the aisle. Suddenly the car jolted violently as a result of a dynamite blast.

"They've gotten into the express car," Charity speculated accurately. "We've got to hurry."

"Y—yi-yi-yi-yi!" a hefty robber keened.

He stood in the shattered roll-back door of the express car, arms upraised, with gobs of paper currency clutched in both fists. Another joined him.

"Come on, Joaquin. There is much money here."

Joaquin dismounted and rushed to join his followers. Quickly they filled their pockets, some mail pouches from the floor, and stuffed more gold coin into saddlebags. A holiday mood pervaded the dimly lighted car; acrid fumes of the dynamite hung heavily in the close air. The men laughed and jostled one another. Before long they had it all. Joaquin led the way to the gaping hole, where he jolted to an astonished stop. In an instant his companions piled up around him.

"¡Hijo de tu madre!" Joaquin exclaimed. Hands filled with bags of money, he and his followers faced a semicircle of ten heavily armed, grim-faced men.

From their midst stepped a young woman, a Colt Bisley competently held in her hand. Joaquin blinked in disbelief and licked his lips. "Wha' you doeeng, woooman?" he demanded in his poor English.

"We've come to put an end to your outrages," Charity answered him in smooth, Sonoran border Spanish.

"Impossible," Joaquin snapped. "Do you know who I am?"

"No. Not that it matters. If you make a funny move,

we'll blow you to doll rags."

"I am Joaquin Murrieta," young Joaquin stated proudly.

"*Pues sí,*" Charity responded sarcastically. "And I'm Queen Victoria." Then she commanded the bandits in general. "Put down the money and raise your hands. *¡Muy pronto!*" she barked for emphasis.

Alas for poor Joaquin the Younger, he still didn't know anything about Charity Rose. He dropped the bags and made speedy moves toward the holstered brace of pistols at his sides. When he did, Charity shot him in the chest.

Joaquin staggered back and pulled one heavy Colt from leather. Charity shot him again in the chest. Immediately ten more muzzles belched flame and smoke. Bandits screamed and moaned, fell to the floor of the express car and thrashed in agony. From not far away came the hurried sound of accelerating hoofbeats as the surviving outlaws, designated as horse holders, escaped the slaughter.

"*Por dios,* I am killed. And . . . by a woman," Joaquin said before he died as ingloriously as his namesake.

Long shadows reached from the pines, fingers pointing east. Concho Bill Baudine, dressed to the nines, stood in a classic pose, one arm extended to point out the storage sheds and other building improvements on the hillside claim. His deep baritone voice rumbled with sincerity as he told of the bountiful production to be enjoyed from this paragon of mines.

"I say," a distinctly English upper-class accent interposed. "If that's the case, why isn't the owner working it now?"

Baudine affected a downcast, solemn expression and clapped one hand over his heart. "He is no longer with us. Not long after he lost title to the mine in a game of cards, the distraught and impoverished man killed himself. Since the gentleman who won the mine prefers to make his living with the pasteboards, instead of hard toil, he sold the mine to me. As a financier and speculator, I hardly wish to undertake such an effort. And so, I am able to offer it to you for a truly handsome price."

"I appreciate your generosity, Mr. Holoburton, believe me I do," Concho Bill's mark responded sincerely. "And I greatly fancy the appearance of the mine. It's only . . . well, I should like to have an assay sample run. Oh, not that I wish to imply that I don't believe you," he hastened to say.

"Of course not. One can't be too cautious in money matters, eh, your lordship?"

"Ah, my good fellow, you do understand. Well—ah—yes."

"We can go inside now if you like," Concho Bill urged.

"Rather close to nightfall, isn't it?" Lord Ramsford suggested.

"Not at all. We can go down to the tunnel head where the largest vein is currently. You can take your sample and we will still have half an hour of daylight to return to town."

"As you wish," the Englishman acquiesced.

On the ride to Sweetwater, Lord Ramsford expressed his surprise at the thick strata of blue-gray rock that sparkled in the carbide light with its rich deposit of silver. Nearly pure, he decided as he used a small pick to hack out some twenty pounds of ore and put it in a tow-sack.

Then he brought up the matter of mining techniques.

"I gather this is rather like coal mining, what?"

"More or less," Concho Bill allowed. "Only the rock is a lot harder. You'll need a good powder man, the best-quality drill bits and plenty of willing workers."

"Ummm. Where do I engage experienced miners?" the nobleman inquired.

"Look around you. Every day a dozen or more prospectors give up the idea of striking it rich and want to go to work for someone else. Most of them are well versed in the sort of mining that is done around here."

"That's encouraging, to say the least. What sort of safety equipment do you employ?"

Concho Bill gave him a quirk of his lips and a conspirator's wink. "Not much. The men are knowledgeable enough to look out for themselves for the most part. Other than a steam engine on the ore hoist and elevator, and carbide lamps like these, we don't use anything at the Lucky Strike. No reason to go to unnecessary expense."

Once in town, Baudine steered his mark to the Tivoli Palace. After a couple of sherries, Concho Bill gave the high-sign to Della Terrace, who came over with another of the establishment's painted ladies. Baudine made careful note of the thorough examination Lord Ramsford gave the engaging young whores.

"Della, my dear, this is Cyril Abbercrombe, Lord Ramsford. Della Terrace, Cyril."

Lord Ramsford had already risen; now he took Della's hand and brought it to his lips as he bowed deeply. He kissed it and muttered in a low voice, "Charmed, my dear."

"Why thank you, y-your Lordship," Della managed to get out. "I'm delighted, also."

"Cyril is going to buy the Five Hearts mine from me," Concho Bill informed the young ladies, giving Della her clue as to what would be expected of her.

"Wonderful. That means you're going to be the richest man this side of Virginia City," Della burbled.

"I rather think he already is," Baudine provided more ammunition for Della.

Cyril Abbercrombe cleared his throat in embarrassment. "I—ah—say, that's a bit of a boast, really. Would you ladies join us for drinks and dining?"

"It will be my pleasure," Della accepted, her eyes locked on the peer's.

Less than half an hour after the cheeseboard had been cleared from their table, Cyril had signed an agreement to buy the mine and delivered a fifteen thousand dollar "good faith" deposit to Concho Bill. The next instant, Della had the young lordling on the way upstairs to her room. There she closed the door behind them and sighed dramatically.

"I've never made love with a lord before. What should I do?" she asked in a low, seductive tone.

"You can get out of that contraption you're wearing, pop into bed and make ready for a little rumpty-dumpty, what?"

"A . . . little . . . rumpty-dumpty."

Cyril took her in his arms and kissed Della soundly on the lips. Their tongues flirted with each other while their fingers made fast work of the fastenings of their clothing. Della encircled Cyril's rigid shaft and stroked him soundly, rubbing the sensitive tip against her silken belly. He groaned at the ecstasy it brought him and lifted her into his arms.

With a strength heretofore unsuspected, he carried

Della to the bed and placed her upon it. She braced her feet flat on the turned-back sheet and spread her legs wide. Cyril joined her and insinuated his hard, knobby body between creamy thighs. With a confidence that came from experience, not class, Lord Ramsford penetrated her moist and steamy cleft and drove deep within her tightly gripping, elastic passage.

Whirled away in euphoria, Della used every trick in her vast repertoire to drain Cyril. He surprised her in that he endured through a third and a fourth magnificent coupling. She found herself getting as much pleasure as she gave. When at last Cyril left her room, he had a big, sappy smile on his face. He poked his head back inside and gave a promise to return the next night. Then he started for the stairway.

He was grabbed by three of Baudine's toughs. One clapped a hand over the struggling Englishman's mouth. Quickly the trio hustled him down the back stairs and away from Sweetwater.

CHAPTER 7

Peace had settled over the Daylight Express, which trundled down the line again as though the robbery had never happened. The law had left, after many questions, and a new conductor had been rushed out from the nearest division point. Charity and Josh sat in the dining car, drinking coffee. Her expression clearly indicated how incensed she remained over the manner in which the county sheriff had conducted his investigation. After a prolonged pause in conversation, she put her feelings in words.

"He talked *at* me. I might as well have been a flighty schoolgirl. That's the way he treated me."

"I've not known you long, Charity," Josh replied in an attempt to be tactful. "But don't you think you're reading too much into it?"

"*I'm not!*" she responded vehemently. "'Now then, Mr. Blaine,'" she mimicked the lawman's voice, "'after you finished off the bandits in your car, you took charge of the other men and led the attack on the remaining robbers?'"

"You were right there and heard me tell him that it was you who organized our resistance."

"Oh, sure, Josh. And he looked at me, then back at you, blinked and said, 'Then it must have been you, Mr. Blaine, who shot that young Rodriguez fellow, who called himself Joaquin Murrieta.'"

"I set him straight on that, too, didn't I?" Josh protested.

"Only he didn't listen to a word you said. When I demanded a claim on any reward money, he just laughed and pat-patted my head like I was a child. Do you want to bet on whose pocket that bounty money winds up in? It won't be yours or mine. Damnit, I had a right to that reward."

"Take it easy," Josh advised, amused by her frustration. "By the way, what was that you showed the sheriff?"

"My badge and commission letter from Graham County, Arizona Territory." Charity's voice changed, lowered. "I'm a bounty hunter, Josh."

"You . . . are? I—ah—wondered how you had come to handle a gun so well, but I never had an idea . . ."

"That a woman would be in that business," Charity finished nastily. "Did that make me suddenly grow horns and get warts on my nose?"

Josh took his time in appraising the pleasant aspects of Charity's figure. Delightful curves in all the right places, a firm, if not large, bust, heart-shaped face, with not too severe a pointed chin, a well-shaped head with dark auburn hair that hung in graceful waves a bit above her shoulders.

"Nooo," he answered as though in a daze. "There's nothing, not the least bit, wrong with the way you look."

Charity's mood changed, became impish. "Why, thank you, sir. At least there's nothing wrong with your vision."

"Rather pleased with ourselves, aren't we?" Josh teased.

Suddenly contrite, Charity spoke urgently. "Oh, Josh, I didn't mean for that to sound snotty. It's just . . . the damned injustice of it all."

"You take this bounty hunting serious, don't you?"

"Of course I do. It goes back to . . ." Charity carefully edited her past for Josh's benefit. "To when I decided to avenge my father's murder."

"Who did that?"

"Concho Bill Baudine and his gang of border ruffians," Charity replied. "My father was sheriff of Graham County. He'd captured Bill and some of his followers and held them in the Dos Cabezas jail until they could be transported to Bisby for trial. The rest of the gang stormed the jail a few days later, killed my father and broke Bill out of his cell. So—I went after them."

"Did you catch them?" Josh prompted, enthralled by this unusual tale.

"Some of them. Baudine's still on the loose. So are some of those responsible. After the first year of hunting men, I discovered that I—ah—liked what I was doing. That's enough about my problems. What takes you to Sacramento, Josh?"

"I'm not stopping there. There's millions in silver coming out of the ground around Virginia City. I hope to make my fortune there, too. You see, I'm not from a wealthy family, even though I'm traveling first class," he added with a note of embarrassment. "I've put everything I have into this prospecting venture."

"It's risky," Charity observed. Then she smiled, warmly and quickly. "Though I think you've got what it takes to make a success."

"Thank you."

"What does your family think of this?"

Josh looked at Charity for a long moment before making his usually unspoken admission. "I'm an orphan. I never knew my parents. Abandoned as a baby and raised by the Sisters."

Charity's face underwent a rapid change into lines of concern and sympathy. "Oh, I—I'm sorry."

"Don't feel sorry for me."

"But I do," Charity blurted in confusion, "and I don't. I suppose you could say I'm an orphan now, too. My mother died when I was born."

Impulsively, Josh took her hand and held it tightly in both of his. "Then us orphans had better stick together."

Charity found it easy to produce a smile. "That will be easier than you think. I'm going to Virginia City also."

"What for?" Josh stumbled out.

Another sweet smile, without any hint of condescension, came forth. "Surely you've read the lurid accounts of rampant outlawry in the Virginia City area? That means rewards posted, and that's how I make a living."

"Ohmygod," Josh gulped. "I—hadn't thought of that."

Their eyes met, then strayed to gaze appraisingly at each other. Charity found she liked what she saw. The earlier violent action had not afforded her an opportunity to take in his features. Slender, and obviously agile, based on his performance during the fight, he looked to be some two or three years older than she. His sandy blond hair grew thick and curly. And he had an engaging smile.

"I'll add to my earlier appraisal. You'll not only do well, I think you can definitely take care of yourself," Charity told him.

"It's my turn to be flattered." Soft gray eyes sparkled under his heavy brows.

Charity noted that his cheeks were somewhat hollow, giving him a brooding look. His obvious interest in her, beyond her prowess with a gun, she found to be reciprocated. This trip, and the future, might hold some excitement for her that didn't involve a lot of gunsmoke.

For all its unfriendly treatment of people who lived along its right of way, the Union Pacific spared no amenity for those who rode in the luxurious Pullman sleeper cars and took their meals in the lavishly appointed dining cars. Rattan fans, operated by colored porters, moved the still air inside, reminding the far-traveled of the exotic colonial extravagance of India and Singapore. Heavy silver graced snowy linen tablecloths; uniformed waiters glided about with laden trays; even the rattle and crash of the rails had been banished from these posh places. At first, Josh Blaine ogled this opulence, then viewed it as mundane.

He experienced another emotion which blinded him to a lack of enthusiasm on the part of the object of his attention. He began to wax downright romantic, yet his embarrassing lack of social position and money put a curb on how much he dared reveal of his feelings.

"We'll be in Virginia City tomorrow," Josh stated the obvious as they dined together late the second night out from Sacramento.

"Yes. And then you can start making your fortune."

"And you, yours," Josh added, a bit down at heart. "I wish you wouldn't risk your life like that, Charity. You're much too beautiful to take such chances."

"What has looks to do with capturing badmen?" Charity stated simply.

"Y-You'd—you'd . . . If anything happened to you, you'd deprive the world of such great loveliness," Josh stammered out.

"My, Josh, that's so eloquent and gallant for you to say. I—I'm afraid I quite underestimated you."

Josh beamed. He signaled their waiter. "Another bottle of wine," he ordered. "I'm only speaking the truth," he told Charity.

"I'm flattered and pleased. But now . . ."

"Now let's drink the wine and talk of more peaceful things. Later we can go out on the observation platform and look at the stars. These mountains are beautiful at night."

"Have you been through here often?" Charity inquired.

"We used to take the Walker Trail through this way for the season in California," Josh answered cryptically.

"'The season?' I thought you must have grown up in an orphanage."

Joshua flushed pink. "I did, for ten years. Then I ran away and joined a traveling circus."

Releasing a trill of laughter, Charity patted his forearm. "You're teasing me, Joshua."

"No I'm not," Josh answered hotly. "It's true. I could not stand any more ear-twisting, nose-pinching and knuckle-rapping by the nuns. That's to say nothing of the

77

whippings we got with a leather strap. Around about eight years of age I made up my mind that I'd never give them the satisfaction of seeing a tear. I never cried again, and all it got me was more severe punishment more often. So I ran away one night when the circus was leaving town."

"Josh, you're serious," Charity spoke her realization. "I'm sorry I laughed. Go on, it's fascinating."

"Well, it didn't go like I'd expected it at first. For a couple of years they used me for just about everything, except a sex object. Not that some didn't try *that*, female and male. I was the wild boy for a while, naked in a cage with dirt under my nails, fur stuck to me by spirit gum, long, shaggy hair, the works. Then I was a geek for six months."

"What's a geek?" Charity asked, not certain she wanted the answer.

"You sure you want to know?" Josh asked through a blush. At Charity's hesitant nod, he sighed and went on. "I bit the heads off live chickens for the amusement of the rubes."

"Awk, that's disgusting," Charity blurted.

"I thought so, too. I was eleven at the time, going on twelve. By my next birthday, my rapid advance in aging was difficult to hide, even with a loincloth, because my voice was changing. They got another geek and I joined an acrobatic troupe."

"How'd you manage that?"

"I'd always been what they call 'double-jointed.' I could bend and twist myself into the most impossible-looking positions. To amuse myself, and get away from my troubles, I used to go in the big top after the show and walk up a guy-wire head over heels. The headliner of the

78

acrobats saw me and the next thing I knew I was in the show. That went on for most of four years."

Eyes alight, Charity clapped her hands. "Amazing. What did you do after that?"

"I left the circus when I was seventeen. It was in Texas and I became a cowhand. Made two drives to Colorado and one to Montana. Then I signed on as a scout for the army."

Completely enthralled by this account, Charity prompted him further. "How did you get to California?"

"Up until a year ago, I was with Crook on the border in Arizona. Those Apaches are a little more Indian than I care to fight."

"It's a wonder I didn't run into you somewhere. I've lived in Arizona since the summer I turned five. General Crook has camped on land owned by a family friend, the Thorntons."

"Maynard and Paulette Thornton? Yes, I knew Mr. and Mrs. Thornton."

"Why—why, I was engaged to their son—Tom." Charity's voice caught as she recalled Tom's bloody death at the hands of Concho Bill Baudine's gang.

"Tom's dead, I hear," Josh said quietly. "He was helpin' some gunfighter named C. M. Ro—"

Charity's gaze dropped to the table. Through a tightened throat she gave the answer she felt certain would end their friendship. "Yes, that's right, Josh. C. M. stands for Charity Moira. A bounty hunter, not a gunfighter, but me all the same."

"My . . . God." He swallowed with difficulty, licked his lips. "It's a small world, Charity. Smaller than we ever guess. I meant no offense. It's just . . . Tom wasn't . . ."

79

"Any kind of gunfighter. How right you are. And I tried to tell him so; still he insisted. Twice they got him. The second time he died. I wanted to die, too. It's . . . taken a long time to get over that. I'm not so sure that I have yet," she quickly added as she wiped at a stray tear.

"Did it have anything to do with this Concho Bill Baudine?" Josh asked quietly.

"Yes. And that's why I want to find Baudine . . . and kill him."

"You couldn't find a better mining property, except of course the Lucky Strike. Why, this mine yields nearly as rich as the Comstock Lode in Virginia City did back in seventy-six to seventy-eight," Concho Bill Baudine rumbled with enthusiasm.

"That's a pretty large claim, Mr. Holoburton," a fresh young mark responded. "Thirty-six million dollars is a hell of a lot of silver. I've heard this latest boom is on the verge of being a bust."

"Nonsense, my good man," Baudine poured on the syrup. "Malcontents and losers who couldn't find color if it up and hit them in the face are behind those rumors. The Five Hearts is solid, sir, absolutely solid. If I didn't have my hands full with the Lucky Strike, I'd develop it myself."

For an hour Concho Bill Baudine had been extolling the virtues of the same mine he had sold to Lord Ramsford a week earlier. Nothing had since been seen of the young English peer. Baudine knew it to be safe for him to offer the property again, particularly since the title transfer had never been filed. He wanted his buyers to be a good deal more callow and ignorant of mining operations than Lord Ramsford.

"I'll tell you what I'll do. I have a friend," the mark informed Concho Bill, "who is a mining engineer. I'll send for him, let him give me some idea of its value."

"Well, now, no need to rush into something like that. Let me consider my offer. What say I take five thousand off the purchase price? Provided, of course, you close the deal today."

Brow gullied in contemplation, the soon-to-be victim weighed this new proposal. "If you can provide an abstract of the title, and past production records, I— might consider that."

"Another fifteen hundred off . . . and that's the best I can do," Baudine offered, sweating.

"It's mighty attractive. I'd still want to see the abstract and production records. Then I'll consider closing the deal today."

"Fine, fine. The production records are in my office in town. I'll have to send for an abstract. Only take a few days. Why don't we ride into Sweetwater now?"

"All right with me," the mark agreed.

By the time the pair reached Baudine's office, he had primed his sucker for the request of "good faith" money. The daily, weekly, and monthly tally sheets told a glowing story of a mine steadily increasing in output. A sure sign of yet a bigger vein to be uncovered. They should be exciting, Concho Bill thought. He'd paid Cassius Varney enough to forge them. The mark grew excited, showed signs of agreeing.

"The abstract will take some time," Baudine repeated, stalling. "The land office in Virginia City is running way behind. It's been next to empty for nearly eight years.

Some of the filings are in distant places. Due to the new, mad rush to file claims, they might take as much as five or six days."

"I can understand that. No one believed another strike in the Virginia City area at first."

"Well then, if everything meets your satisfaction, what about a good faith deposit, say two thousand against the purchase price?"

"Done, Mr. Holoburton. I'm much encouraged. I'll go to the bank for it now."

After the prospective owner of the Five Hearts mine departed, Concho Bill allowed himself a satisfied smirk and then rose from in front of his roll-top desk. "Better get over to see Cassius Varney about that certified abstract," he muttered to himself on the way to the door.

CHAPTER 8

Grotesque, unfeathered necks extended, the ugly, red-wattled, yellow-beaked heads canted downward, the soaring turkey buzzards kept beady-eyed watch on the events below. So far they had found nothing attractive, no rotting flesh, not even some creature near enough to death to warrant their attention. Less than eight months ago, only a handful of the big, two-legged beings inhabited the ghost town that had once been Virginia City. The carrion birds had endured slim pickings for a long while since the mines closed down. Now the increase in human activity promised a more substantial larder.

Keen senses operating at maximum efficiency, the buzzards located an object worthy of closer examination. They swooped low, circling, drawing closer to the thick scrub in a narrow gulley in a fold of the foothills south of Silver City. They drew nearer. There it was, a rotting corpse, in prime condition for their feasting.

Landing, they waddled, like drunken sailors on fat toes, to the odorous bundle that had once been Lord Ramsford, and contentiously began to feed. Lord

Ramsford, it soon became obvious, didn't mind at all. To the north of them, in Virginia City, the eastbound from Sacramento arrived and life went on as usual.

From a window of the Pullman, Charity Rose observed that Virginia City bustled with activity of all sorts. Prospectors led mules down the street, wagons came and went. Several enterprising businessmen had workmen applying fresh paint to their establishments. A line stood outside a small, unattached building with a huge sign that identified it as the assay office. A less pretentious billboard advised: "File claims at Land Office, 210 Grant."

Gold fever ran high, Charity knew from the sensationalist newspaper accounts. As a rule, gold- and silver-bearing ores could often be found close to each other. Usually one predominated to the point of not making it worth mining the other. Virginia City had made its name as a silver bonanza. That knowledge led Charity to doubt that much gold would find its way to the smelters. Accompanied by Josh Blaine, she left the Pullman to tend to her horse and dog.

Josh hovered around her like an anxious suitor. Over the days and nights of their passage, he had soundly fallen for the lovely redhead. For all her longing for Jeremy Ortiz, Charity Rose found herself developing a fondness for the attentive young man.

"When will I see you again?" Josh asked as the loading ramp swung into place at the stock car.

"I'm not sure. You're set on finding the mother lode, and I have my own plans. No doubt I'll remain in Virginia City. When you are in town, Josh, look me up. I'd enjoy your company, and we can always have a late-night supper together."

"I'd—like that very much," Josh gulped.

"Then, I suppose this is good-bye for now," Charity concluded as the depot handler led Lucifer down the ramp.

"Where will you be staying?" Josh pressed.

"At the best hotel in town."

Well versed in Virginia City and its environs, Josh responded brightly, "That would be the International Hotel. I read where it had never closed after the first boom died out. Almost as fancy as the Palace in San Francisco."

"Then that's for me," Charity advised with a warm smile. She gave him a cordial kiss on one cheek.

After Charity arranged for Lucifer and Butch at the livery stable, she located the International Hotel, the third and largest of that name, which had opened in 1876 at the height of the bonanza. Although a bit tarnished, and worn at the edges, the International had every right to claim kinship to the famous Palace in San Francisco. The glories of its large, ornate lobby, although faded, remained impressive. Charity engaged a room on the third floor and oversaw the bellboy who handled her modest amount of luggage.

Once inside the third-floor, corner room, the lad deposited her bags and turned smartly, one hand extended. Charity gave him a silver dollar. He bobbed his head in thanks, pleased that at least this guest knew things cost more in Virginia City. He started out the door, then paused on the threshold.

"If you're gonna be doin' business outta your room, I can steer the best gentlemen customers to you for twenny percent of your take."

"I'll be doing nothing of the kind, you little imp,"

Charity said hotly.

"Don't tell me you're not a fancy gal," the youngster challenged.

"I am not," the heat came again.

The pre-teen produced a knowing grin and cobalt eyes sparkled above the writhing freckles high on his cheeks. "Then what are you?"

"If I told you, you wouldn't believe me," Charity fired.

He paled suddenly and lost his wise-guy expression. "You're not a schoolteacher, are you?"

Charity laughed lightly. "Good heavens, no."

"That's good." The boy's plucky nature returned. "Whatever, I can still fix you up with anything you want. . . ."

"I'll—ah—keep that in mind."

With a nasty snicker, he gave Charity a big wink and darted out into the hall. Charity closed the door and rummaged in one of her two portmanteaus. Quickly she changed clothes, into the garb of C. M. Rose, bounty hunter. In the process she paused long enough to admire her smooth, clean-limbed body in the tall, oval, bevel-edge peerglass mounted in a walnut stand. She made little of the few thin, white scars that marked her torso, momentos of her years of seeking vengeance on Concho Bill Baudine. With her tan outfit properly in place, she felt ready to make a visit to the local law.

"Della, you've not been doing right by us lately," Mattie Orcutt stated in her husky, whiskey-baritone voice.

Weak sunlight filtered through the lace curtains in the

madam's office at the Tivoli Palace. Outside, the muted sounds of daily routine in Sweetwater attested to the constant ebb and flow of prospectors, mine employees and the shiftless parasites who lived off them. From a distance a couple of gunshots broke the undertone of voices, hoofs and wagon wheels.

"How do you mean, Miss Mattie?" Della Terrace asked meekly.

Mattie shook her long mop of hennaed sausage curls and a hot glitter came to her pale blue eyes. "Oh, I think you know exactly what I'm alluding to."

Della tugged at a stray wisp of corn-gold hair and blinked back the tears that threatened to fall from her wide, troubled blue eyes. "But I don't, I really *don't*," Della pleaded.

"Mr. Descoines has given you the high-sign three times lately to slip a Mickey Finn to certain customers, and you failed to do it," Mattie charged, her buxom cleavage aquiver with indignation.

"I—I must have misunderstood. Or I didn't see him pass the signal."

"My, how careless we are," Mattie Orcutt drawled sarcastically. Then her tone grew harsh, rasping. "I think not, my fine miss. Word is you're getting too friendly with certain customers who are slated for a—ah—trimming. You'd best be minding your chickens before you break some eggs."

"Why, it's simply not true," Della defended herself.

"Bull," Burt Kill rumbled from one side, where he leaned a beefy shoulder against the wall. His bull neck and bullet head combined with thick shoulders to give him an appearance of tapering to a point instead of having clear-cut features. "You ask me, I think you should turn her over to me for a little lesson in loyalty."

Della shuddered. She knew from other inmates of the bordello about the evident pleasure which Burt Kill derived from the vicious application of his "lessons." One girl, she had been told, had died of his particular attentions. It proved a costly mistake, for which his superiors had compelled Burt to exercise less zeal. She bit the inside of her lower lip to compose herself and again attempted to mitigate her guilt.

"I've got no one special among the regular customers. I honestly must have not seen the signals. Although I'm an independent, on my own hook, I realize I must do what is asked of me in this place. Please understand my simple mistake and I promise not to do it again."

An unholy light gleamed in Mattie Orcutt's washed-out blue eyes and her stingy mouth pursed in a wet, red bow. This one always flaunted her being freelance. She'd given in all too easily, Mattie speculated. Perhaps she did need a lesson in penitence.

"Burt, take her down to the cellar," Mattie purred. "Introduce her to your friends. Be careful, though. Don't leave any marks that might reduce her earning power."

Burt uttered a sound somewhere between a whinny and a snort and reached out one big, ham hand to take tight hold of Della's arm. "Yes, Miss Della. I'll do that, I surely will. You come with me, gal, and don't give Burt no trouble."

Della realized resistance was beyond her ability. In sudden horror, she also admitted that from this point on, she had lost her independent status and would never be allowed to leave the Tivoli Palace until her earning days as a fancy girl had gone by. She would be a prisoner from now on, every bit as much as the other girls. Her new knowledge brought forth a sob as she and her captor neared the door to the cellar.

"None of that, now," Burt crooned. "You'll like my friends. They have black, shoe-button eyes, nice, soft gray fur and long, skinny tails. But most of all, they have long, sharp teeth."

Della screamed when Burt shackled her wrists to chains fastened into the wall. She screamed again when she saw the first rat. A third howl of terror came from her when Burt held up the furry monstrosity and it bit her under her bare right breast. She didn't stop until she went hoarse, long after the little nips stopped coming.

Charity found only the jailer in the marshal's office. Marshal Donovan and his deputies were out with a posse and not expected back for several days. That gave her time to look around the reviving town. She purchased several needed items, enjoyed excellent meals at her hotel and read local accounts of the outlawry that threatened to become epidemic. The posse returned three days later, dust- and mud-smeared, exhausted and empty-handed. A message came around to her hotel. The marshal would see C. M. Rose the next morning.

U. S. Marshal Donovan received C. M. Rose with mixed emotions. He welcomed anyone who might aid in rounding up the overflow of hardcases making his job so difficult and dangerous. Yet, he still had a lawman's dislike of bounty hunters. The young C. M. Rose seemed cut of a different pattern. Polite, alert and deferential, with a deputy's badge and letter of authorization. He decided to reserve final judgment until he'd seen Rose's performance.

"So you've come looking for troublemakers?" he

prodded gently.

"That's right, Marshal. In particular I'm interested in any of the men known to ride or to have ridden with Concho Bill Baudine."

"Any particular reason why you think Baudine and his gang should be around Virginia City?" Marshal Donovan asked.

Rose produced a fleeting smile. "You acknowledged that the lawless element came close to matching the honest folk. And where money runs so freely as in a boomtown, I figure Concho Bill would seek it out as an easy source of profit."

"Good reasons by my book. Virginia City is calming down some. I've good reason to believe this last bonanza is a flash in the pan. Most of the wild sort have moved on already. There's not been twenty thousand found around here. The only place holding its own is the latest big strike along Sweetwater Creek. The Lucky Strike mine is pulling a lot of silver from the ground, shipping it through here to Carson City.

"A few sourdoughs have struck good color. And Lord knows there's enough gamblers, sharpers, soiled doves and the like around to attract the hardcases. There's been enough robberies and killings to spawn a whole drawerful of wanted bills. You want to find the wooliest of the badmen, they can be found around Sweetwater Creek and the town that's grown up there."

"Where do I find Sweetwater Creek, Marshal?"

"About forty miles south of here. I'll provide you a few current flyers and you can try your luck. Believe me, you're going to need a lot of that."

After thanking the marshal, Charity set off for the livery stable. There she purchased a pack horse at a price

that would elsewhere provide a matched pair of
champion pacers. In her mind she ran over what she
would need to outfit herself for an expedition to
Sweetwater. Given what she had paid for the sway-backed
pack animal, she wondered if she had money enough to
cover her purchases.

Dust, and the acrid smoke of exploded dyamite, hung
in the air. A long, shallow layer of the hillside had been
blown down into loose gravel at the base of the slope.
Josh Blaine had worked this isolated site over the last
four days without results. Unlike his fellow prospectors,
he did not join the grimly determined throng along the
banks of Sweetwater Creek.

He had chosen a tributary, a narrow stream that
meandered through an eroded fold in the hills, and began
to examine what appeared to be a promising formation.
He mopped sweat from his brow with the grimy sleeve of
his flannel shirt and worked his way up over the talus to
where a vein of rock had been exposed. When he grew
closer, excitement clutched at his heart. There it was.

A wide band of blue, clayish rock had been exposed by
this last, largest blast. Eagerly, Josh hefted his pick and
began to break away big flakes of the malleable material.
It looked like granulated lead—that much he had learned
from books on prospecting. Silver, in its natural state,
rarely came in the form of nuggets. In these blue-gray
strata of pitchblend, it formed threads of varying size and
density that wound through the clay.

Eons of time and pressure had transformed the once
soft material into a consistency only slightly less solid
than sandstone. Josh worked at his discovery for nearly

an hour before he stopped and began to examine the huge flakes he had broken away.

After checking several of his first pieces, he knew a growing elation. He found a few granules of a dull, metallic substance that grew more plentiful from one side of the flake to the other. Quickly he grabbed another. More, yet not enough to make it worthwhile. His last five specimens set his heart to pounding, hands trembling. Swiftly he turned to the face he had been working. Eyes wide, Josh examined the exposed vein.

It started low down, extending upward from left to right. At the point where it disappeared into the hillside, it had reached a width greater than his forearm. Josh could no longer contain himself. He let out a bellow of triumph and began to swing his pick in a frenzy. He'd struck it rich!

Josh began to lay his plans, his jubilation hiding the fact he did so aloud. "First I gotta get an assay sample. Enough to really show the worth of this strike. The claim's already marked, but I've got to go into town and file it and register my assay. Rich as this is, I should have some money left over from the sample to buy part of the mining gear I'll need. Oh, this is a beauty, a real beauty."

When he had what he considered a generous assay sample, Josh threw down his pick and rummaged through his kit for something in which to carry the ore. He came up with two gunnysacks and hastily filled them with the rich deposit. He tied the mouths of the bags and then fastened them together to form crude saddlebags. After saddling his horse, he slung the precious cargo over his mount's rump and swung aboard. Humming a scrap of some vaguely remembered hymn, Josh set off for Sweetwater.

Two men unwound from their sitting positions and mounted up as Josh disappeared around a bend in the stream bed. "That feller's got him a regular bonanza," one observed.

"Sure does," his partner agreed. "We'd best get into Sweetwater and let the boss know. He'll want Buck and the boys to move in and take this one over. Looks richer than the Lucky Strike."

It took only a few minutes for C. M. Rose to discover that Sweetwater held the prize among boomtowns for sin and corruption. Sharpers, gunfighters, hardcases of all sort hung out in the raw little community. Standing like Colossus among pigmies, the three-story Tivoli Palace dominated the skyline. Its white, clapboard exterior glowed like polished marble. Although it was not yet noon, a steady stream of patrons converged on the establishment. C. M. walked Lucifer in that direction to the unsynchronized music of half a dozen pianos, two guitars and a percussion section provided by the rasp of saws and bang of hammers.

"Mo'nin, suh," a white-jacketed, wool-headed colored man greeted C. M., halted at the black-painted logging chain, suspended between two iron posts, that served as a tie-rail. "Y'all come fo' dinner?"

"Uh—yes," Charity responded. Her husky, raspy voice aided Charity in her disguise at close quarters.

"He-he, yassah, an' maybe a little pokey-poke on the side, huh?"

There was no mistaking his crude, two-hand gesture with circled thumb and forefinger and rigid middle digit. "Could be," Charity falsely informed the doorman in an

93

offhand manner.

On the inside, Charity quickly became convinced that this "social club" represented the heart of Sweetwater. The huge common room, which occupied most of the ground floor, rose the full three stories and more to large windows of clear and stained glass that let in sunlight in pleasing patterns. Crowded with tables, most of them filled by prosperous-looking businessmen, who rubbed elbows with miners and prospectors, the oversized hall buzzed with low conversation. White-coated waiters worked through the throng, with trays of drinks, elegant-looking platters of roasted partridge, venison—even a suckling pig—and covered dishes she could only guess at. A good number of women were present, though not what could be considered wives and dowagers of the community.

Soiled doves, Charity recognized at once. The wings that extended off the central hall contained gambling devices, bars, and more ladies of the night. Charity reasoned that if she wanted to gather information on illegal activities, the Tivoli Palace was the place. She could hardly invade a whorehouse as C. M. Rose, so another tactic would have to be employed. In order not to attract unwanted attention, she found a small table to one side and ordered a modest meal.

After her brace of fried squab, duchess potatoes and dandelion greens, Charity left the Tivoli Palace and located the livery stable. "I'd like to have a place for my dog to sleep," C. M. Rose informed the hostler.

"How long you figger to be in Sweetwater?" the stoop-backed old man asked.

"At least a week or two."

"Ummmm. Big dog. Must eat a lot," the taciturn

liveryman observed. "Say six bits a week—in advance."

"Fair enough," C. M. agreed. "Be sure to grain my horse every day. I may want him at a moment's notice and for some hard riding."

"Kinda young for a tin-horn gambler, and ya don't dress like a messenger boy. What sort of business would call for a fast, well-fed horse?"

"I rob banks," C. M. answered facetiously.

"Tend to doubt that," the hostler's brief, but to-the-point, observations continued.

"The truth is I'm looking for wanted men."

"Bounty hunter, eh? Figgered you had somethin' to do with lawin'."

"Do you have a problem with that?" C. M., annoyance growing, demanded.

"Me? Nope. High time we get a little law and order in this town."

"Then here's your money. I'll not be around for a couple of days. Thank you very much."

Charity set off to locate a headquarters for C. M. Rose. She found a small, quiet boardinghouse on a side street that would fit nicely. She brought her C. M. Rose clothing and equipment in a large carpetbag and settled in. Then she changed into a comfortable travel dress, high-top shoes and a parasol. With her small Colt Lightning in her purse, Charity Rose left C. M. Rose's room and headed for the stage depot. She would return to the Tivoli in a few days, she determined, as another person.

CHAPTER 9

Josh Blaine heard the music of every bird and thrilled to it. He'd been even luckier than he believed. Fantastic, the assayer had informed him. The vein, provided it turned out to be a large one, could make him a millionaire several times over. His sample assayed out at over one hundred pounds to the ton of ore. He paid all filing fees, the assay bill and had enough money left over to throw one mind-shaking whing-ding. The peaceful sounds of nature decided him on how to do this.

First he bought some fine, new clothes, suitable to a prosperous mine owner; then he strolled down the bustling main street of Sweetwater to a saloon named The Emporium. There he bought drinks for the house and helped himself to the free lunch counter. Accustomed to men with a lot of money to spread around, only a few inquired into the means of his new wealth. To them, Josh put on a wise and crafty expression and spoke softly.

"Sold a producing mine for a bundle," he lied smoothly.

A fool and his money, most of them considered

philosophically. They had seen all that before. So most went off to seek other excitement. Josh soon grew bored. He recalled the exhilaration he had experienced in the presence of that lovely, but deadly, young woman, Charity Rose. He wanted a woman, Josh realized. The best place to take care of that problem, he had heard, was the Tivoli Palace. Bestirring himself from the barfront at The Emporium, Josh headed toward the fabled gaming house and bordello.

It took no time to find himself in a small room off the communal hall, seated at a tiny table, a silver wine bucket and a lovely young woman beside him. Sighing in contentment, he swished the bottle of champagne in the rapidly diminishing ice, wrapped a towel around it and poured another glass for himself and his companion.

"I love champagne," the girl simpered. "The bubbles tickle my nose."

"They do a lot more to me, Fleur," Josh observed.

"They're supposed to put lead in your pencil."

"They do, as I'm sure you've found out. My problem is I don't have anyone to write to."

"Oh, you do now, lover. Believe me you do. When do you . . . want to go up to my room, Josh?"

"When we finish all this, and I've got the shakes so bad from wanting it that I can hardly walk."

"Honey, you came in here that way."

Disconcerted, Josh's expression changed to one of concern. "Did it show that badly?"

A trill of laughter, which Josh considered better music than what the birds made, answered him. "Josh, the only time I've ever seen someone with a worse case of the hornies than you was once long ago when a man brought in his kid, a boy about thirteen, to get it for the first time.

He thought it might cure the boy from playing with himself."

"Did it work?" Josh asked, joining in the humor.

"I don't know. I doubt it did any good at all. We made the chimes ring five times that night and the kid left me with his dingus still stiff as an iron bar. Ummm. More champagne."

"I can't imagine it being a long time ago," Josh said gallantly, although a bit slurred. "You couldn't possibly be more than twenty-three."

"*Ullp*." Fleur gulped down a long draught of the wine. "Missed by a year, and it was nine years ago this next February. Let's hurry and get this fancy stuff out of the way. Talking about love makes me get the shakes."

"Sure, I meant what I said earlier. You're very lovely. And I picked you out of a crowd of beautiful girls."

"Thank you, kind sir." Fleur tipped her glass for more champagne.

"Can we have someone bring this up to the room? We may need to renew our strength from time to time."

"Attaboy! Plan ahead, I say. I'll ring for a waiter and then we can get down to what's important."

When the waiter arrived he handed Josh a folded slip of paper. "A note from Mr. Holoburton, sir."

"Thank you. Would you send this up to the lady's room, please?"

"Certainly, sir."

Not knowing Holoburton, Josh assigned no importance to the message and shoved it in his suitcoat. Arm-in-arm with Fleur, he climbed to the second floor on the ornate staircase and they strolled along the inner balcony, with its elaborate wrought-iron railings, like those of the Vieux Carré in New Orleans. Inside Fleur's

98

room, they undressed quickly, without the need for conversation. Josh smiled in pleasure at the exquisite body she revealed to him, and Fleur's eyes widened at the rich endowment Josh had received from nature.

"It's easy to see you're not a thirteen-year-old," she murmured as she stepped into his arms and brought her lips to his.

They made love in a frenzy the first time. Josh drove deep into her, expending months of pent-up energy that left them both panting and slippery with a sheen of passion sweat. While they waited for nature to take its course and invite them back to the feast of Eros, Fleur began kissing his lean, hard body.

"Tell me," she asked between kisses. "Do you have any family with which to share your obvious good fortune?"

"No, I don't. I'm an orphan."

"Oh, poor boy. It must be . . . so lonely."

"Somewhat. Ummmm, that's good."

Fleur cupped his cods in her palm and gently manipulated them. Her lips found his navel and bussed it soundly. "Then you have no one who knows where you are, what good fortune you've encountered?"

"None at all. No, there's one person. A young lady. She knows I've gone prospecting."

Her lips nuzzled in the thatch of sandy pubic hair at the base of his rising organ. She kissed the shaft. "Is your find a new one?"

Josh sucked air in sharply between clenched teeth as she skillfully worked fingers and lips up the length of his manhood. "Yes. I've only today filed claim and registered the yield."

"Are you going to work it alone?" Fleur asked as she

straddled him and lowered her facile tongue over the sensitive ruby tip of his member.

"Aaaah—aaah! For a while I will. When it comes to sinking a tunnel or anything like that, I'll have to hire help."

Fleur changed ends and lowered her moist, ready cleft onto his throbbing phallus. Slowly, teasingly, she took him in. Josh moaned and filled his head with pictures of someone else giving him such utter delight. Someone with burnished copper locks and a sweet, heart-shaped face. Someone named Charity Rose. He nearly reached premature completion as the fantasy grew.

"I don't believe this," Fleur gasped some two hours later. "Six times and you're ready for more?"

Josh gulped down more champagne. "I will be in a moment."

His rapid elongating phallus testified to that. Fleur's right hand found it and began to stroke. When this monumental session ended, she would, she decided, have a lot to tell Frenchy Descoines.

Heads turned when she entered the swank surroundings of the Tivoli Palace. Hair teased into a gossamer bubble, with a daring dress that featured a split up one side and the lowest décolletage most of the patrons had ever seen, Charity Rose returned in disguise. She believed she would get a great deal more information under the protective cover of a painted lady. Walking a bit unsteadily in the high, spike heels of her calling, Charity made her way to the end of the large, main bar.

"I'd like to see whoever is in charge of the girls," her husky voice informed the barkeep.

"That'd be Mattie." He made a sign to one of the

plentiful bouncers. "I'll get her over here for you. Would you like a drink while you wait?"

"Sure. Only none of that tea you pass off as whiskey when a girl is working. A glass of sherry. The—ah—Christian Brothers if you have some."

"Comin' up," the apron replied cheerily. "You know your stuff, all right," he added as he poured.

"It's the best made in this country. Spanish sherry has a funny taste."

"That it does. They transport the barrels in the ship's bilges and saltwater seeps in. Here you go."

"Thank you. How much?"

"On me," the bartender offered, groping in one pocket for a coin.

"Thanks again."

A buxom woman with a stout, barrel body bustled up to the bar. She twisted her small, cruel mouth into an approximation of a welcoming smile as she eyed Charity. "You wanted to see me?"

"Yes. I thought I might be able to work out of your place."

"Hmmm," Mattie stalled. "Mattie Orcutt. That dress of yours will knock 'em dead. You have any more like that?"

"No. But I have a couple of net outfits with tights and lace ruffled skirts."

"That'll do, honey. Shows you've been around. Folks that work around here call me Mattie. Let's go to my office and I'll explain the rules."

"Lead the way, Mattie."

Inside the madam's sanctum, Mattie got down to business at once. "Take a seat. You haven't told me your name."

Charity had avoided that because she hadn't thought

of one to use. "Uh—sorry. I'm Mildred Hanson," she supplied, using the name of a schooldays friend. "I've been using Mimi."

The frosty, insincere smile returned. "We already have a Mimi. How about Francine?"

"I don't feel like a Francine. Would Gigi do?"

Mattie's cold blue eyes lighted. "Gigi it is, then. Now, here's how we run this place. Bar girls, who only hustle drinks, work from eleven in the morning until nine at night. They are paid two cents on every drink they get a customer to buy and five cents on any the customer buys for them. Our fancy girls work from one in the afternoon to eleven at night. They make four bits on every trick they turn."

"I can't be bothered for less than fifty-fifty," Charity stated simply.

Mattie Orcutt cawed her version of laughter and patted a pudgy palm on her desk. "Honey, those purple prose romance books from London may call it a pearl beyond price, but there ain't a one worth that much."

Charity let a little anger glow through. "I'm an independent. I don't have an Uncle John, or a Cousin Bob, nor anyone else I have to support. I wasn't 'turned out' in your house, and I'm not your whore. I make my living on my back, *and it is my back,* remember that. You have a lot of overhead, and I can understand that—a place like this. Ordinarily I wouldn't offer more than ten percent to a bellboy in a nice hotel. Only around Sweetwater I don't see many bellboys, or nice hotels. So, I'll split with you. Otherwise, I walk right now."

Mattie restrained an urge to bite at a thumbnail. "Now, don't be hasty, Gigi. I'll have to take it up with the man who runs this whole place. He takes a cut of what I take.

102

Truth is, we don't have a real redhead. Just some henna jobs. Be nice to have the real goods. Why don't you come back, say one o'clock, ready to work, in case he says yes."

"I can do that," Charity said shortly.

Done up as Gigi, Charity Rose returned to the Tivoli Palace at the appointed time. Mattie greeted her with a lopsided smile. "It's agreed, on one condition. We've got a couple of other independents here, who are giving up a lot more than you. I want you to keep quiet on what split we're making. No need for those girls to get high-minded ideas."

"I can accept that," Charity gave generously. "When do I start?"

"Right now, sort of. I'll take you around and introduce you to the bartenders and the boys at the gaming tables. That way they can recommend your qualities to our gentlemen customers. Now, a few rules that you'll be expected to abide by.

"First, no drinking real booze when you're working. Also I don't allow the girls to use opium, laudanum, loco weed or any other drug at any time. The customer is always right. You do whatever he wants you to do. For the frills you can charge extra."

"Sounds reasonable enough. Just what sort of 'frills' do you allow?"

"About anything, but no whips or anything that would scar the girls. But if someone wants you to dress up like a sheep and go baa-baa, you do it."

Charity gave her a quizzical look. "Are you joshing me?"

"Not a bit. I had a place in Santa Fe. Old sheepherder

103

came in about once every three months. He'd stuck it to so many sheep he had to have what he was most familiar with. Had a new girl, little bit of a thing, just breaking her in. She didn't mind crouching on the bed with a sheepskin and . . . but that's another story. Come with me."

Mattie put on quite a tour, Charity had to admit. She met the gamblers, barmen, waiters, some of the other girls and several regular patrons. The varicolored light from the stained glass fell in patterns across the green baize of the card tables and sent showers of sparkles from the wheel of fortune. Although she had no way of knowing that Concho Bill Baudine's partner, Frenchy Descoines, owned the Tivoli Palace, she was astonished at the number of men working there who had been with Baudine at one time or another. Coincidence? Charity doubted it. She made it through her first shift without incident.

She hustled a few drinks, talked with a number of men, yet managed not to have to go upstairs with anyone. Tired, footsore, she departed from the opulent bordello at eleven o'clock. Her hotel room and bed felt wonderful.

Cassius Varney had outdone himself. Concho Bill Baudine gloated over the excellence of the spurious abstract he presented with a flourish to his doubting mark. "Here you are. As you can see, Doane Phillips sold to Cyril Abbercrombe, Lord Ramsford, who sold to the Lucky Strike mine—ah—me, Victor Holoburton. And now I am prepared to accept the balance of your payment and transfer title of the Five Hearts to you."

"Ummmm. Please, you understand that I'm not

suggesting anything might have been irregular. One must look out for one's best interests, eh?"

"You find the abstract satisfactory?" Baudine prompted.

"Oh, yes, certainly. We can go back to the bank now and arrange for the transaction."

Concho Bill made his face into a study of regret. "I'm afraid you'll have to attend to that on your own and meet me at my office later. I have—ah—other commitments this morning."

"Very well, Mr. Holoburton. I'm sure I can manage that. You'll have the transfer deed and all the proper papers ready later today?"

"That I will." Baudine produced a fleeting smile. "Now, if you will excuse me?"

"Until later. Say, three o'clock?"

"Four-thirty would be better," Concho Bill suggested.

By then the land office would be closed and the filing delayed until the next day. And before tomorrow, the mark would be taken care of by Buck Harris. Quite a satisfactory day's work. Concho Bill Baudine climbed into his surrey with a thought toward his next appointment out in the field.

There would be no slip-ups. The men who had discovered an anemic vein of silver believed they had negotiated a shrewd bargain, gaining twenty thousand dollars for a worthless claim. In so doing, they would accomplish what no one else had been able to do. They would put one over on the mighty Mr. Holoburton, owner of the Lucky Strike. They'd take their money and run, while Concho Bill Baudine had some of Gerd Meeker's men salt the paltry claim with a good grade of silver ore from the Lucky Strike. Then he could sell the worthless property for ten times what he paid for it. Yes, a good day, indeed. Then on to the next project.

How long before he would be able to have Harris's claim-jumpers move in on Joshua Blaine? The young whelp had struck a truly rich vein of silver. Better in many respects than the Lucky Strike. Baudine wanted it badly. The first problem remained finding the claim. So far Harris's band of cutthroats had failed in this. Perhaps he might prevail where so many had failed.

Time and patience would tell. Before long, though, Joshua Blaine would be feeding the scavengers and Bill Baudine would own his mine.

CHAPTER 10

Sullen rumbles sounded from the surrounding hills. Huge piles of black-bottomed, gray-white thunderheads rose along the western horizon. The birds had grown silent. Here and there a tardy scissor-tail swallow or sparrow sought a niche to settle into. People went about casting frequent, dubious glances at the gathering power of nature. On the afternoon of her third day working at the Tivoli Palace, Charity Rose hurried toward the tall, alabaster edifice glad that she had brought along a parasol.

This weather, she considered, would produce one of two extremes. There could be little business. Which she saw as an advantage; she would have time to gather more information about the huge sporting house and its customers. Or the place would be packed full of men who could not work in a thunderstorm.

Either way, she thought gloomily, her ability to stay out of the clutches of the amorously inclined patrons would be sorely tested. The idea of going to bed with a man she did not know, did not like, and did not care to please made her skin crawl. Unbidden, memories of that terrible day when Concho Bill Baudine's gang came to free him from her father's jail welled up to drive all other considerations from Charity's mind.

She fought off the sensation of revulsion and shame the images produced and set to preparing a series of glib, inoffensive ripostes to turn men's lustful thoughts away from her body and onto something else. While she contrived her set pieces, she skirted the front entrance and proceeded along a narrow, flagstone walk to the back door.

"Aftahnoon, Miss Gigi," greeted the middle-aged black man who tended the door and worked other times on the yard and garden. "We's in fo' a real gulley-washer this time."

"What makes you think so, Cato?" Charity replied, liking the smiling, gentle handyman.

"Them clouds big enough to contain half de ocean," he observed. "Don' rain much ovah here, but when she come, she be a gusher."

"Better have your slicker handy then, Cato."

"Oh, I's do, Miss Gigi. Least it be ovah befo' de night through."

"For that, I'll be thankful."

"Cook fixin' roast' ducks an' Texas deep-pit brisket fo' tonight's menu."

"Ummm," Charity murmured with genuine pleasure. "Save some for me, will you?"

"I'll do dat."

In the small, narrow crib assigned her, Charity changed into her saloon girl outfit, a dark green one of the net tights and frill-skirt variety. She rolled her long, auburn locks into a single, large coil, which she secured

108

in place to one side of her head with a collection of glazed porcelain butterfly pins of Japanese origin. Her high-heel, calf-length, cross-lace shoes glowed like polished obsidian. She snapped open a Mexican-made, tortoise-shell fan and covered all of her face except the hypnotic sea-green eyes and high, smooth forehead. She blinked long, false eyelashes into the mirror and moved her body sinuously.

For a moment she considered adding a feather boa to the ensemble. No, she decided, that would definitely be gilding the lily. A sudden, pure erotic surge passed through her. For the first time she admitted to herself that she enjoyed dressing up like a strumpet. From her street purse, she took a short-barreled .38 Colt Lightning and put it in her sequined clutch purse. Ready now to face the eyes and hands of the customers, she left her second-floor room and started for the staircase.

Low and appreciative, a whistle followed her along the hallway. Light and graceful, she descended the treads, drawing more admiring glances and soft comments. A tremendous white flash above the glass dome of the rotunda broke all movement into jerky, stuttering images. Although still daytime, the sky turned a sickly black-green. Several of the soiled doves squealed in fright, but not Charity.

Aloof, like a queen or at least a princess, she gave each man an intimate glance, smile or wink, yet seemed not to tread in the same universe with the rugged men of the silver fields, nor even the fancy-dressed dandies of town. The volume of the deluge grew louder and elicited nervous remarks. Five hard-rock miners vowed they had fallen instantly in love. Each vied with the others to buy Charity her first drink of the evening. She allowed the

109

most lecherous of the quintet that privilege.

"Miss Gigi," he stumbled over his tongue, "you're the most lovely, the most beautiful, the most . . . most I done ever came upon. Why, I'd give up ever'thing for just one of your smiles."

"Oh, how eloquent," Charity cooed while long, forked streaks of silver and blue flickered outside. "I don't ask so much of anyone. You've bought me a drink, for which I am grateful." She inclined her five-foot-four height on tip-toe and kissed him soundly on the lips. "That is for your kindness. Now I must drink and run, must meet my public, you know."

"Say you'll come back?" he pleaded like a love-sick swain.

"Oh, I shall. There's a lot of night ahead of us. . . ."

With similar innuendo, Charity managed to deftly turn away the offers of engaging her services through the afternoon and most of the evening. In one corner of the large common saloon, five men sat at a table. Their tough, horny hands identified them as working miners, every bit as much as their too-tight, ill-fitting, shiny suits and black derby hats, begrimed by gray dust finger marks.

"And it's far certain sure the Mollys are comin'," Conrad O'Farrel was saying as Charity approached. He cut off his narrative the moment he saw her lovely form. A scowl replaced the earnest, excited expression he previously wore.

"Ah, sure an' I've died and gone to heaven, for here comes an angel to give me succor," one of the others at the table piped up.

"Aye, the Lord knows yer a flatterer, Brian Killabrough," the man next to him despaired.

"I am flattered, and I'm pleased," Charity returned. "Yer all true sons of the ald sod, *taim cinnte?*"

"*Ta an ceart agat,* you are right indeed, me lovely *cailin,*" the beaming young Irishman responded. "Brian Killabrough at your service. Will ye join us for a wee drop?"

"Na-na, Brian, we've much to talk about. Another time, an' that's a fact," O'Farrel admonished in a commanding tone.

Charity left them to spend a few moments with other patrons. Her cheerful appearance and willingness to trade anecdotes or jesting insults with the customers warmed their hearts to her. The second and last storm swept through shortly after eight o'clock. The scent of fresh, rain-scrubbed air filled the vast common room. People's moods lightened. Charity began to float purposefully through the evening, rather than drifting aimlessly. This being a weeknight, most of the miners, employed by the Lucky Strike or two other large mines, began to drift out early. By ten-thirty, only a few townsmen and ten independent prospectors remained. Charity considered herself fortunate once more.

Until a narrow-headed, rodent-faced dandy with over-large yellow teeth and terrible breath latched onto her arm. "C'm here, you beautiful thing. I've been waitin' all evening to get to paw you."

Stale whiskey blended with the fetid odor of rot that emanated from his ugly, thin-lipped mouth. A shaggy line of ill-kempt mustache writhed like a worm on his upper lip as he made kissing sounds and shoved his head close to her face. She had no trouble in recognizing him as Dapper Dan Evans, who had ridden with Concho Bill Baudine at the time of her father's murder. His tiny, deep-set eyes glittered with the black malevolence of a cornered rat.

"I've got money, and plenty of it. I'll be takin' you up

111

to that room and you can haul my ashes for me."

"I—ah—it's close to my time to get off," Charity answered lamely.

"Don't mean nothin'. I've got more'n enough for an all-nighter. Let's go, purty thing."

Ponderous waves of revulsion washed over Charity Rose. For all her skill in evading such a circumstance, she now found herself caught in a dilemma. She dare not refuse or she would jeopardize her cover. Worse, she feared that if Evans sobered some he might recognize her. For a wild moment, Charity sought some means of escape. In the end, her hatred for Baudine's scrofulous henchmen overcame her disgust.

"All right," she snapped after a good five minutes of his unwanted attentions. "If you'll stop pawing me." An idea bloomed. "Get us a bottle, too. I'm about to gag on that cold tea they give us girls for whiskey while we work. If you're up to it for all night, then no one will ever know the difference."

"Hey, I like a little sneakiness in a gal. Shore enough, purty thing, I'll get the jug right now."

Evans half dragged Charity up the stairs. In her room, he yanked the key from her hand and turned it in the lock. "We ain't goin' nowhere until the rooster crows. Git outta them clothes and get ready for the best humpin' you ever got."

"That'll be the day," Charity murmured to herself.

"Huh?" He gulped as he pulled the mouth of the whiskey bottle from his lips.

"I said I can hardly wait."

"Your heart goin' pitty-pat? Those furry little lips getting all twitchawe?" His hands closed around her chest, thumbs rubbing into the thin cloth across her nipples. "We're gonna get these hard as peach stones,

112

sweet thing."

Dan Evans let go suddenly to take a long slug on the bottle; then he began to feverishly divest himself of clothing. He had a pallid, unhealthy cast to his skin, his chest completely hairless, with prominent blue veins close to the surface. He sported several scars that Charity knowingly considered to be the result of knife fights. His knees were knobby, legs scrawny. When it came to that member he loudly proclaimed he anxiously wanted to exercise, its entire length lay hidden in a thick thatch of curly black pubic hair.

Perhaps the vast quantity of alcohol he had consumed prevented him from reaching a state of excitation quickly, Charity considered. But, as he stared at Charity, he started to get hard.

All in all, Charity observed, he wouldn't even be competition for Corey Willis, her thirteen-year-old lover of so many years ago. Had she been looking forward to this, she would have been terribly disappointed. As it was, she was merely indifferent. She noted Dan's faraway, glassy stare and an idea of how to resolve this predicament blossomed in her mind.

Slowly, trying to simulate seductiveness, Charity removed her clothes. Dapper Dan Evans ogled her. Charity felt cheap and dirty. She beckoned him to the bed and sat him beside her.

Her fingers closed around his stubby manhood and began to manipulate him. With the other hand, she caressed his belly and rubbed his chest. Then she urged another drink on him. He squirmed on the edge of the bed and then lay back, sighing in contentment. Charity continued her distasteful task.

Why did something that could feel so good with one person be so awful with another? She increased her

113

efforts, hoping to draw him to a climax. Dapper Dan groaned and panted and humped his pelvis. Gradually his groans softened, grew longer, blended one into another, and changed into snores.

Sodden with liquor, Dapper Dan Evans lay beside her, his phallus limp and unresponsive, his breathing regular and deep. Charity had had enough. She got away from him as from a timber rattler. She spat dryly in disgust and went to the small glazed ceramic pitcher and basin to wash herself.

Hands dripping and faintly scented by the harsh lye soap, she still felt unclean. She dried herself and sought her clothing. She hung every garment in place in the curtain-fronted plank cabinet and reached for her street clothes. A knock sounded at the door.

"Go away," Charity mumbled, allowing herself to be miserable.

"Gigi, it—it's me, Della. Let me in."

A resurgence of spirit elevated Charity's mood. She shrugged into a bulky dressing gown and hurried to the door. Della entered with a rush. Her eyes were large and expressive, mouth turned in a moue of disapproval. She gave Charity a quick hug and held her out at arm's length.

"You poor thing!" Della blurted. "That Dan Evans is a pig. He always gets sloppy drunk before he picks a girl. And then there's nothing he can do anyway. You want me to help get him out of here?"

Charity gave it quick thought. "No. Let's lay him out on the bed and let him sleep. He'll wake up thinking he's had a grand time."

Della suppressed a giggle. "Good enough for him. That's about all he can do the best of times—*think* about it. I—I came to talk to you because you're an independent, like me. I want to get out of here. But I'm

114

afraid of Burt Kill. He's bone-mean, and enjoys hurting girls. He—he whipped me on Mattie's orders. When I first came here. Another time he used rats to—to do awful things. I'd like to stick a knife in him," she ended darkly.

"I don't intend to be here much longer," Charity confided.

"Oh, why not?"

"Della, I—I have to trust someone. Things are not exactly as they appear. I'm not a—ah—working girl."

Della studied Charity closely for a long, silent moment. "I can believe that. Matter of fact, this is the first time I recall seeing you come upstairs with any customer. And you . . . look familiar to me, somehow. Do you have a relative, a young guy about your size, named C. M. Rose?"

Charity began to chuckle softly. "Della, I wondered how long it would take you. Remember C. M. Rose telling you he was really a girl?"

"Then you're—you're C. M. Rose?" the young prostitute gulped.

Charity nodded. "I'm he, or he's me; sometimes I don't know which. The point is, I came here to learn more about wanted men. I intend to round up a few and collect the bounty. There's another reason I have to leave here soon," she went on, changing the subject before Della could probe too deeply.

"What's that?"

"I've noticed a number of men working here who used to be in a gang run by a man named Concho Bill Baudine. Dapper Dan here is one of them, also, though he doesn't work at the Tivoli. Sooner or later, one of them might recognize me. Have you ever seen a man around here who looks like . . ." Charity went on to describe Concho Bill

Baudine, including his shiny conchos, velvet vest and flowing mustache.

"No," Della answered quickly. "I've seen everyone who comes here more than once. Nobody like that has ever been around." She had no intention of deceiving Charity. After all, Mr. Victor Holoburton wore expensive suits and was clean-shaven.

"Okay, Della. All the same, I've got to leave here soon. Right now what I need is a place to sleep."

"You can use my room. It's got two beds in it."

"Wonderful, Della. We'll let Dapper Dan sleep it off and go away well pleased with himself."

Early morning brought the sweet-pungent scent of damp sage, resinous greasewood and the clean, fresh odor of the ponderosa pines. The previous night's heavy rainfall had turned to frost before morning, the shaded areas still hoary with white. Joshua Blaine had eaten a meager breakfast as the sun rose, and now set about the task of exposing more of his vein of silver.

It appeared that he could strip-mine this rich deposit. That would eliminate the necessity of tunnels, shafts and stopes, and the expensive shoring they required. Joshua soon worked up a sweat and removed the heavy flannel shirt he had donned in deference to the chill air. His muscles rippled as he swung a pick, breaking off large hunks of blue-gray clay. In each, the small granules of silver, dull gray as lead, showed clearly in a band nearly four inches wide. The ample thread of precious metal grew more abundant with each slab broken off. So intense did he become, Joshua failed to hear the soft clop of horses walking into his camp.

116

"You there," a harsh voice broke his concentration.

Joshua glanced over his shoulder and saw seven men clustered in the center of his diggings. Ever mindful of the chance of claim-jumpers, Joshua dropped his hand to the smooth, walnut grip of his Remington revolver as he began to turn around. He'd cleared leather when the first of Buck Harris's brigands fired and missed.

Young, with quick reflexes and keen eye, Joshua pumped his first bullet into the chest of one claim-jumper, cleaning him from the saddle in a spray of blood. Joshua dodged and leaped to one side, firing again, without result. Four of the outlaws had their weapons in action by the time Joshua found temporary shelter behind a mound of ore.

His sweaty body registered the slamming impacts of hot lead against the opposite side of the mound. His lack of confidence in this apparently flimsy cover drove him into the open again. He expended his last two rounds, pleased at the yelp of pain from a wounded man. Then sudden fire raged in his side, staggered him and left his head vulnerable to another bullet that creased his skull.

Bright lights exploded in Joshua's head, followed by a growing numbness that brought on dizziness and nausea. He dropped to his knees, blood streaming down his waist on the left side, with more running past his ear and washing over his right cheek. He never heard a third shot, nor felt the fiery slug that grazed the back of his gunhand.

"That finished him," Buck Harris pronounced. "We'll get some boys here in the next couple of days to take over his claim. Damned rich, too. A good morning's work, boys."

CHAPTER 11

A scream awakened Charity Rose. Blackness engulfed the room in the Tivoli Palace. At first, Charity thought she might have been the one to scream. Lately her nights had been filled with disturbing dreams of her degradation and rape at the hands of Concho Bill Baudine's gang. Then she heard it again. Following it came a bass rumble. Charity blundered out of the strange bed and painfully barked a toe on a chair leg.

"Wa'issit?" Della Terrace muttered thickly.

"I don't know," Charity made terse reply as she remembered where she was and why she slept in Della's room.

She located her Colt Lightning and held it in a firm grip. At the door, she paused a moment, then turned the key and opened the thin portal a narrow crack. The first thing she saw was Burt Kill's thick shoulders and bull neck. Then beyond him, cringing against the wall, one of the girls. Charity recognized her as Paulette. While she watched, Burt advanced on the helpless girl and swung a powerful arm.

His slap cracked loudly in the hallway. Paulette screamed again. "Please, she blubbered. "Please don't hit me, Burt."

"You're holdin' out," Burt accused. "I been watchin' an' askin' questions. Them johns payin you extra in the room an' you're keepin' it."

"No, that's not so. Oh, sometimes a man'll give me a dollar 'cause he's pleased, but no re-real money."

Burt's ham-hand balled into a fist and he smashed it into Paulette's face. From where she stood, Charity could hear the thin bone in Paulette's nose break. Blood splattered on her face. Paulette screamed again, a thin, gurgly sound.

"You hurt me, you bastard!" She tried to scratch Burt.

Burt hit her in the nose twice more. Paulette doubled over and Burt kneed her in the face. She slammed back against the wall, groaned and shuddered. Licking his lips, Burt hunched his shoulders and started for her. Something cold and hard touched the nape of his neck.

"Touch her and I'll blow your neckbones out through your gizzard," Charity Rose said icily.

Burt froze, hands open and upraised. Charity made a shooing motion to Paulette. "Go to your room. Lock the door."

Recognizing the voice of the girl he knew as Gigi, Burt let out a roar, "You bitch!"

With lightning speed, he spun, swatting at her extended arm. Charity had more than enough skill to prevent an accidental discharge of her Colt .38. Regardless, it flew wide from her hand and Burt appeared to swell in front of her, menacing her with his fury.

Only for a moment. White froth at the corners of his mouth, he sprayed spittle as he mouthed obscenities.

Then he started for her. Charity dodged him and scurried to retrieve the Colt Lightning. She swung it back and he stared, cross-eyed, down the black hole of the muzzle.

"One twitch, you son of a bitch, and I'll blow your brains out the back of your head," Charity snapped coldly.

"I'll break you like I did all the other bitches. Then I'm gonna fuck you until your belly aches."

"I'm a freelancer, remember, Burt? I don't belong to Mattie Orcutt or to this goddamned whorehouse. You lay one hand on me and you're dead. Now, take me to Mattie."

Muttering curses, Burt led the way to Mattie's luxurious suite on the third floor. The madam had not retired when they arrived. She wore a feathered gown that closed at the neck, and small silver slippers with diamonds sewn into the pattern of tiny squares. She sat on a Victorian version of a Roman dining couch and sipped champagne. Her fingers held dark smudges from the chocolates she had been consuming.

"What's this all about?"

"Your pet animal tried to punch me up, Mattie," Charity growled. "We had an agreement. See that this asshole lives up to it, also. Keep his hands off me, keep him out of my sight, and make him treat the girls a lot more gently, or I'll put six little holes in him so fast he won't be leaking from the first by the time I start to reload."

"Who the hell do you think you are?" Mattie bellowed as she sprang from her lounge. "This is my place and I give the orders around her. You were lookin' for a place when you found this one, and you can be lookin' again damned fast. I ought to let Burt have you to do with whatever he wants. And put that gun away. I hate those horrid things."

"That figures," Charity snapped sarcastically.

"Now get this straight. You will not ever again threaten Burt with a gun. If you do, you'll not live to see another day. Another thing—what Burt does to the girls he does at my direction. You will mind your own business or you might wind up with some broken bones. Now, get out of here. . . . Ah, what are you doing here anyway?"

"I had a late customer," Charity answered simply.

"That doesn't matter. Get out and keep your nose clean . . . or else."

Back in Della's room, Charity told her what had happened. In conclusion, she added, "In the next couple of days, I'm leaving here all together. If you want to come along, be ready at a moment's notice."

Della thought of Burt and shivered. "I will. I'd like to give Burt a good solid kick before we go."

"If he gets in our way, I'll give him a grave," Charity promised.

Sound and light were interchangeable. Giant insects buzzed inside his head. For a long while, Joshua Blaine lay there on his back, unable to move even a single finger. He felt hot, then frightfully cold. Try as he might, his eyelids would not open. His tongue, partly protruded from his rictus-stretched lips, had swollen to fill his mouth. For a moment he knew he was a man and he knew he was alive.

Then blackness came—huge, surging waves of velvety darkness that lifted, whirled and consumed him. Vaguely, he heard the weak, far-off tinkling of bells.

Slowly he sank into the void, toward a tiny white spot. The dot enlarged, grew brighter, swelled until it achingly filled the whole inside of his head. And Joshua heard the angels sing.

Constantly watched, after the incident of two nights ago, Charity had to do more than go through the motions of her supposed job. Three times, so far, she had "entertained" a gentleman in her room upstairs. Fortunately for her, the first had been a young man her own age, a bit shy and uncertain about his first experience with a lady of the evening. He had long, black hair, the bluest eyes Charity had ever seen, and a Welsh name.

Ian Llewellen had big hands, huge feet and a complete lack of knowledge in the realm of sex. Warming to his reticence, Charity found herself becoming aroused. It made the encounter so much easier. In less than fifteen minutes she had them both disrobed and she began kissing Ian in intimate, stimulating places. His nervousness soon abandoned him and he produced an exquisite erection that performed with credible valor.

Charity soon found herself lost in a welter of passion. Ian learned quickly and they completed their long, energetic encounter in a state of bliss. Downstairs again, her face and body radiant from the superb loving, she soon had another erstwhile swain. She made several sincere attempts to turn his interest elsewhere, then resigned herself.

Her new customer proved more knowledgeable, and experience led them to whoopingly joyful satisfaction. Albeit, Charity harbored a sensation of emptiness throughout the entire performance. Her third compulsory coupling occurred the next night. It turned out rather like her ordeal with Dapper Dan Evans.

Not quite so onerous, she soon discovered. Although unable to maintain a fine, solid erection, her john at least retained his keen senses and responded delightfully to her touch, tongue and facile lips. Now she found herself in a situation far less pleasant than any of her previous engagements.

Her john on this night, fresh from cleaning up after work, was no other than Gerd Meeker, general manager of the Lucky Strike mine. That he was a large cut socially above the others who had known her in two nights, proved no consolation. For all his social graces, Charity soon found a rotten core within.

"What's all of that?" she demanded when Meeker dumped the contents of a large leather valise on her bed.

Meeker shrugged. "A few toys. Mere pastimes to make our night more enjoyable."

Charity looked with distaste at the rough metal of handcuffs, leg irons and a wide collar with a length of chain attached to a ring. She saw a pair of spiked leather gloves, a leather apron, with a prominent hole in the material, what might be a thumbscrew, and three neatly coiled whips. She swallowed back her disgust and turned to see Meeker busily undressing.

"I—ah—told you downstairs that I don't go in for these sort of things," Charity choked out.

"If you work here you will," Meeker answered with blithe self-assurance.

"You're quite mistaken in that," Charity made bold to state. "I don't belong to Mattie Orcutt or this house. I have an agreement with Mattie and it doesn't include these *perversions.*"

Meeker produced a nasty, superior smile. "Maybe we should take that up with the real owner of the Tivoli Palace?"

"Who do you mean? Mattie Orcutt let me work here as an independent."

"Mattie runs the girls. A man by the name of Maurice Descoines owns it."

Struck speechless and immobile, Charity stared at the naked man before her. *Maurice Descoines . . .* Frenchy Descoines. There couldn't be two of them. That meant that Concho Bill Baudine would be around here somewhere. Her mind whirled with the implications. She started to force out words, to reveal her knowledge. Caution prevented it and Charity made herself return to the subject at hand.

"As an independent, I can quit and walk out of here at any time. I'll do so before I participate in such unnatural pastimes as you seem to want. Here's your money," she went on, delving in the décolletage of her revealing dress. "Take it and get out of here."

"Now, see here, I made an arrangement with you. You're by far the best-looking girl in the place. I'm not leaving until I get what I came for," Meeker snarled, anger rising at being thwarted.

Charity grabbed up her purse and pulled the Colt Lightning from it. "Get out or I'll kill you where you stand."

Meeker paled. He had a dreadful fear of women with guns. For that matter, he felt that the world would be a better place for him, Buck Harris and others like them if people weren't allowed to have the deadly things. A gun in the hands of a righteous man was a terrible threat to those who preyed upon him. Moving carefully, Meeker bent to retrieve his clothing.

"All right, I won't argue with a gun. Put that thing away."

"I will after you leave," Charity informed him coldly.

"I'll leave. I'll take my money and go. But you can be sure I'll complain about this to Mr. Descoines."

"Go right ahead. You do that."

Meeker had begun to sweat. "Please, don't point that awful thing at me."

"What? This?" Charity exclaimed as though just aware of the sixgun in her hand. "Why, this is only a toy. A mere pastime to help us enjoy the evening," she mocked him.

Hastily the pallid, portly mine manager put on his clothes and slid narrow, pasty feet into fine, English leather boots. Large drops of fear sweat stood out on his brow and his left eye had developed a tic. Wetting dry lips, he extended a shaking hand for his money.

"I ought to keep this for my wasted time," Charity stated. "But then, the customer should leave happy. You'll be happier, I'm sure, with this than a bullet hole."

"I'm going, *I'm going!*" a terrorized Gerd Meeker bleated.

After he had departed, the reaction hit. The rapid rush of adrenaline, followed by the equally quick let-down, caused Charity to shake so violently she could hardly get the revolver back into her purse. She would have to get word of this development to the law in Virginia City. It would be best if she did so in person.

With that decided, Charity hastily tidied up and made ready to leave her room. She'd sleep in her bed at the hotel tonight and start out for Virginia City early the next morning.

"You say she gave back your money and threw you out?" Frenchy Descoines said in an amused tone. "Quite a spitfire we have. Which one of the girls was it?"

"Gigi. The new redhead Mattie took on. She claims to be working for herself."

"Ummmm. We have a couple like that. Della Terrace is one. I didn't know Mattie had taken on any more. Well, there's not much I can do about it if she is independent. Let's go talk to Mattie."

Elegant in his dark maroon cutaway coat, lace-front white shirt and formal tie, Frenchy Descoines rose from the large, comfortable chair. Without a glance at his visitor, he started for the door. Gerd Meeker perforce had to follow behind.

Out on the ornate third-floor balcony, Frenchy paused at the wrought-iron grille railing as was his habit and gazed proprietarily down on his domain. Impatient, Gerd Meeker joined him and gave only a cursory glance. Then he looked again, where the large, curving stairway wound to the ground floor. Excited, he pointed to a modestly dressed young woman nearing the final treads.

"There she is. That one," Meeker blurted.

Frenchy looked down at the auburn-haired woman, appreciating the soft curve of her shoulders and pleasing bodice. Even with only a top view, she seemed somehow familiar. Then a voice called out from the floor below Frenchy and the young woman turned to look up.

"Gigi! I'll see you tomorrow," Della repeated.

Instantly Frenchy nearly choked. Words sprayed from him in his excitement. "But God, I don't believe it. It's

126

her. Charity Rose."

"She said her name was Gigi," Meeker said lamely.

"None of the girls use their real names. That doesn't matter," Frenchy stated hastily. "What is important is that Charity Rose is here. Right inside this place, working for Mattie. For some twisted reason she was sworn to kill me and Bi—er, ah, Victor Holoburton."

"My God! Sh-She did have a gun. To think, I was in the same room with her. God. You'll have to do something about this," Meeker babbled.

"I will. You can count on that."

Saturday night, Charity thought with annoyance as she left the porch of the Tivoli Palace. That meant there would be no end to the raucous activity until two or three in the morning. All about her, the streets swarmed with tipsy celebrants. They may thank God it was Saturday, Charity considered sourly, but everyone who had to put up with them, from bartenders to dance hall girls, cursed the weekly arrival of Party Night. Street lamps made yellow smudges at block intervals in the dust- and smoke-polluted air. They did little to illuminate the dark recesses of midblock space. Charity started off along the boardwalk, headed to the hotel.

She covered two long blocks, being jostled and bumped by the throng of humanity. A couple of the more daring had pinched her bottom. With each stride the urgency of getting away from the Tivoli, from Sweetwater, grew inside her. Charity crossed a side street, steering clear of a urine-scented mud puddle, and soon walked her way out of the light. That fact had barely impressed itself on her when three men suddenly loomed in front of her.

127

"What . . ." she snapped out, then went silent when two of the strangers grabbed her and one clapped a grubby hand over her mouth.

They dragged her into an alley. Charity's mind spun. At first she suspected robbery; then the fear of rape welled up. Frantically she tried to force one hand into her street purse. Silent and determined, their attention fixed upon the task of getting her off the street, none of her abductors noticed it. Well back in the complete darkness of the alley the trio halted. Slowly Charity's vision adjusted to the faint glow of stars and a silver crescent of moon.

She looked from one to another of her captors. Mouths set in grim lines, they had so far not spoken a word. One of them grabbed her long, auburn hair and yanked her head back, exposing her throat. Another produced a knife. Faint celestial light put a blue flicker along the keen edge. Charity struggled harder, while she thrust her hand inside the purse.

Before she could withdraw it, the man with the knife slashed at her. She managed to bolt backward, reflexively raising her arms to defend herself. A sensation of heat, followed by cold and numbness, radiated up her arm. Distantly she became aware of a warm trickle on her arm.

"Damn," the assassin's harsh whisper broke the silence. He raised his arm for another try at her throat.

Charity drew her Colt Lightning and squeezed off a round. Yellow-orange muzzle-bloom lighted the alley. The men holding her gaped in utter surprise. Her assailant stared at her from three wet, black eyes; then the one between his eyebrows began to bleed. Charity triggered another shot. Hot lead bored into flesh in the notch at the base of his throat. Uttering a soft, gurgling

128

wail, he backpedaled a half dozen steps and fell dead.

Recovering from their momentary shock, the other two tried to unlimber their sixguns. Released from their hold now, Charity crouched and spun to one side as the hardcase she faced put a bullet through air where her torso had been previously. His partner gave a surprised grunt and crumpled to the ground with a wound in the upper right section of his chest.

Stunned for the second time in less than thirty seconds, the gunman could only gape, his mouth forming words that would not come out. Charity hadn't the luxury of time to spare. Her Lightning rapid-fired two cartridges, sending a pair of .38s into the gun-wielding assailant's heart. He blinked, then began a gagging cough that brought up a gout of dark blood. Charity came upright and stood over him, silently considering a safety shot.

His twitching body stilled and the light faded from his eyes, obviating the need for another bullet. Charity turned to the wounded man in time to kick his sixgun away from clutching fingers. She knelt at his side, the hot muzzle of her Lightning pressed tightly under his uptilted chin.

"Who sent you after me?" she demanded hoarsely.

"Go to hell," he squeezed out from pain-contorted lips.

Slowly Charity racked back on the sear notches. With each click, the would-be killer's eyes widened. She poked the Lightning muzzle against his throat.

"Your friend shot you, not I. But I can finish the job."

"No—no, don't. It . . . was Frenchy."

"Descoines?" Charity queried.

"Yeah—yeah, that's right. S-Said to kill you nice

and quiet."

Instinct urged Charity to finish it then, blow the brains out of this paid murderer and find a place to get away. Reason suggested otherwise and at last prevailed against the clamor for safety. She decided to play it smart and disappear for a while. She'd take this one along also. That would leave a lot of unanswered questions for Frenchy Descoines.

"Get to your feet," she commanded.

"I can't. I've been shot."

"If you stay there, you'll be dead," Charity coldly told him. "Now get up and start moving."

"Wh-where are we going?"

"To the livery stable. I'm going to tie you up while I get ready to leave town. Then you're coming with me."

CHAPTER 12

Sergeant Chet Bleaker strode along the main street of Sweetwater. The pale fall sunlight felt good on his massive shoulders. As Chief Granger's second in command, the police sergeant had set out on an important weekly errand. One by one he visited the business establishments of Sweetwater. From each, with the exception of the Lucky Strike mine and the Tivoli Palace, he departed with the scuffed Gladstone bag somewhat weightier than before he entered. While saucy jays scolded from the cornices of raw wooden buildings, Sergeant Bleaker entered the general mercantile. The bell over the door tinkled merrily.

"Be right with you," Melvin Weems, the proprietor, called out from where he wielded dustpan and broom.

"Make it fast," Bleaker growled. "I gotta take all this back to the office before noontime."

Timid Melvin Weems did three things simultaneously. He winched, twitched nervously—which sent the collection of lint balls, dust, and sand flying—and turned pale. His hatred of these weekly payoffs to that ignorant slob of a police chief had reached the point that it exceeded his fear. The time had come, he had decided only the previous night, to put an end to the shakedown. Now he had to fit actions to his ideas.

"Th-then you can go right now and have time to spare. I am not going to pay you anymore."

"What? What did I hear? It couldn't be what I thought it was. No one, not a single soul, is that stupid. Now go over to that cash box, you goddamned marshmallow, and start taking out money," Bleaker snarled.

"I'm not going to do it, and that's final. Get out of my store and don't come back."

To bolster his new-found courage, Melvin Weems hurried behind a side counter and brought out a loaded shotgun. Facing the weapon, in the hands of an obviously frightened and determined man, Joe Bleaker restrained his impulses and put on a conciliatory face.

"I'm sorry you feel that way, Weems. I'm leaving, but I'll never forgive myself if something happens and I didn't warn you. If you're not protected, something dreadful could happen to the store, or to you."

"Are you threatening me?" Weems demanded.

"No—no. It's just that the protection you pay us provides you insurance that nothing will happen," Sergeant Bleaker said, as though explaining to a slow-witted child. "The rowdies will leave you alone and we'd sure stop any hold-up man who chanced to come in here."

"You're paid to be policemen. It's the job of the police to prevent such things as you mentioned."

"Police pay is low. In order to provide the amount of protection required, given equally to every merchant, it costs a great deal more than we're being paid for. But you'll find out for yourself, Weems. If something bad happens, remember what I told you."

Less than an hour after Bleaker's departure, five young rowdies trotted their horses into town. From the conversation among themselves, and the spirited behavior of their mounts, anyone could clearly see they had some serious celebrating in mind. Two blocks from Weems's store, they spurred their horses into a gallop. Hooting and yelling, they charged toward the center of town. Sixguns drawn, they began firing into the air. When they came even with the general mercantile, they methodically shot out the large display windows.

Crouched in fear, Melvin Weems listened to the glass tinkle to the floor. The laughing young men gave a shout and jumped their horses forward, to crash through the destroyed windows and land destructively among the displays of yard goods, work clothes, pickles and other items of stock. Flour, sugar, molasses, pickle and vinegar barrels were toppled over, mingling their contents in a sticky morass on the linoleum floor covering. When two of the rowdies found Weems cowering from the wanton destruction, they dismounted and yanked him from behind the counter.

They continued to hold him while the other three took turns methodically and viciously beating him. They left no part of him unbruised. Several powerful kicks went to his groin. When he became a limp and blubbering wretch, suspended in their grasp, one of the two holding him spoke in complaint.

"Hell, he ain't gonna make it through more. You fellers didn't let me have a turn. That ain't fair."

The apparent leader snickered. "Awh, poor Louie. Didn't get any blood on his knuckles. Tell you what,

Louie. I'll take your place and you punch him a couple of good ones in the mouth."

Louie's eyes glowed. "Can I, Ritchie?"

"I said, didn't I?"

In a scant two seconds, the young toughs had changed places. Louie balled his glove-clad fists and began to smash them into Melvin's slack mouth. He felt something give and a chunk of tooth floated out in a stream of blood. He reached down and tilted the groggy man's face up toward him.

"You awake, old man? Listen good. From now on you pay up your protection dues and you won't get hurt. Know what I mean?"

"Ga-got you," Weems said muzzily. "Wo-won' do it 'gain."

"You better not. That way things like this won't happen."

Released from the youths' strong grip, Melvin Weems fell to the floor. Consciousness seeped from him as he listened to them laughingly lead their horses from his ruined store.

Wind soughed through the tall, stately ponderosa pines with a sound like rushing water. Two people occupied a small cabin, nestled up against the northern face of a granite cliff. Long abandoned until early that morning, the stout building served as an excellent place for the business at hand. C. M. Rose sat at a rickety table, opposite her prisoner.

His red-rimmed eyes held a feverish light and he frequently lifted a canteen to his lips with his good hand. Charity watched him closely. She had bound him to a chair with lengths of rope around his chest and leg irons on his ankles. She waited now while he finished swallowing.

"That wound has to be infected. It's hurting you a lot more than you let on. The sooner you tell me what I want to know, the sooner I'll take you to a doctor in Virginia City."

"Yeah? And then what?"

"To jail. You tried to kill me, remember? I don't let little things like that get past me."

"Wasn't my idea. Burt said we was to do it. We figured you'd be easy, bein' a woman." Beside him, Butch raised his huge triangular head and uttered a low growl. The hardcase shivered and cringed away. "Jesus, lady, can't you take that mutt away?"

"I could, but I'm not inclined to do so. Give me some straight answers or I'll let him chew on you for a while."

"That's crazy!" the hardcase blurted. Then he thought better of it; maybe she *was* crazy. "Uh—I mean, you wouldn't do that to an unarmed man."

"Don't try me. Now, when you say Burt, do you mean Burt Kill from the Tivoli Palace?"

"Yeah," came the sullen answer.

"You and I both know Burt's no great brain. Who gave him the order? Was it Frenchy Descoines?"

"I—uh—I suppose so."

Charity tied a shortcut. "Is Concho Bill Baudine behind what's going on in Sweetwater?"

"I don't know anyone by that name, lady."

At a sign from Charity, Butch reared up on his haunches. His black lips pulled back in a rictus, exposing long, sharp, yellowed teeth. He put a huge paw on the outlaw's thigh. Sucking in a long draught of air, the

135

would-be murderer cringed away.

"But you do know Frenchy Descoines?"

"Yes. He owns the Tivoli Palace."

Charity quickly described Concho Bill Baudine as she had last seen him. Then she added, "Wherever Frenchy goes, Concho Bill can't be far away. That sound like anyone you've seen around Sweetwater?"

"No," the young tough answered quickly.

Too quickly, Charity thought. She raised her hand and Butch took his on-guard position. Her prisoner could not restrain a gasp of horror.

"I'm tellin' the truth, lady. D'you think I'd lie with that monster fixin' to make dinner out of me?"

Charity gave him a cold smile. "Do you know Buck Harris?"

His eyes darted in their sockets like caged squirrels. "We—uh—that is, I used to work for him."

"Used to?" Charity challenged.

"Yeah. I just decided to quit."

"Were you along on the silver robbery and claim-jumpings?"

"I don't have to answer that," the captive spat defiantly.

"Of course you don't. Butch . . ."

"Sure—sure, I—I rode with them."

"That's much better." Charity asked several more questions and then brought the man to the final part of his ordeal. "There's a piece of paper and a pencil on the table. I want you to take them and write a note to Frenchy. Tell him that you and your friends managed to kill me. Put down that one of the dead men shot the other by accident, which he did, and that I killed the other. Say that due to the killings you thought it wise to take my

136

body off to some safe place to prevent any trouble with the law. Then sign it."

Stripped of his last resistance, the hardcase complied. Charity folded the paper, after reading the note, and put it in a pocket. Then she handcuffed her prisoner and freed him from the chair. Outside she helped him on his horse and mounted Lucifer. In silence, they started off for Virginia City.

Clear, bright blue shimmered above. Slowly, ever so slowly, the sounds of insects, birds and small creatures intruded into the former pit of black silence. Fire burned in his side, further awakening him. He knew his name by the time he rubbed gummy crystals from his eyelids and lashes. Head throbbing, Joshua Blaine moved his arms slowly.

With one hand he felt gingerly of the central core of the radiating heat. A thick crust covered the source. Dimly he saw a canteen resting on a low table some distance away. It seemed to take an hour to drag himself there. Each movement unleashing a new wave of pain, he unscrewed the lid and sloshed water into his free palm. With this he bathed away the granules that blocked his vision.

His surroundings immediately reminded him of how he had come to this condition. He had been working; men came, shot him, and left. Or did they? He turned his head to search for them and new agony exploded. When the world around him stopped swaying, Joshua again opened his eyes.

He found himself alone. Field mice and other small creatures had been at his supplies. He could see holes in bags, with wide halos of flour, cornmeal and sugar around them. Joshua tried to stand and made it only to his hands and knees. His skull threatened to split. Not far off his horse remained hobbled, but otherwise free to graze. Melting with pain, he started off toward the animal.

"Easy now, easy, boy," he crooned.

Gradually the distance diminished. Joshua could reach out and touch a fetlock. He crawled a bit closer and got a good hold. Using the sturdy leg for an anchor, he pulled himself to the horse's side. Hand over hand he worked his way upright.

"Good boy, good horse," he repeated while he stroked the familiar neck.

He bent and unfastened the hobble, then gradually guided his mount to where a powder keg stood upright. There he slipped a bit into the horse's mouth. Misery alive in his side, he had to wait long, precious minutes before he could work the headstall over the animal's ears and adjust the reins. He tried to raise a leg and swing up, but failed. With a great deal of searing torment he managed to climb on top of the short barrel of powder. Again he swung his leg up and succeeded in throwing it over the horse's back. Groaning with effort, Joshua pulled himself upright and bent forward to take the reins.

Lights exploded in his head and he reeled dizzily. At last he drove back the vertigo and clapped his heels into his mount's ribs. Each step awoke new torment. After a quarter mile, Joshua began to wonder if he would be able to make it to Sweetwater.

Through slitted eyelids, Concho Bill Baudine watched

the obsequious waiter withdraw from the room. With nearly ritual slowness, the menial pulled the thick double doors together at the middle. God, the furnishings and accommodations for the Tivoli Palace had cost a fortune. Freighted all the way from San Francisco, the luxurious drapes, heavy oak doors, the several barfronts and backbars, chairs, tables and carbide gas light system consumed all but a bit more than a thousand dollars of what the gang had accumulated over several years. It had been worth it, though, Baudine thought. The discreet click of the brass latch signaled a resumption of conversation.

"Gentlemen, I think our progress deserves a toast," Baudine announced as he poured from a chased silver decanter brought in by the waiter on a large silver tray.

"Yes, I agree," Frenchy Descoines added. "We're not far from having complete control of every business in town, except the assay and land offices. It's too bad about that little disturbance the other day," he added, addressing his comment to Buck Harris.

"That damned mercantile owner pulled a shotgun on Bleaker," Harris explained. "Refused to pay his—ah—insurance premium. Bleaker acted on his own to have the boys convince Weems to cough up."

"Bleaker's your man, Wade," Concho Bill reminded the chief of police. "You know we've agreed to avoid outward shows of force. If I've learned anything over the years, it's that too much rough stuff draws the attention of the law. You should have sat on Bleaker, arranged some sort of less—ah—public demonstration. Perhaps a small fire, late at night?"

"Which would probably have burned down an entire block," the head lawman in Sweetwater said grumpily.

To him, Baudine's idea of discreet lacked something. To his surprise, Baudine admitted to error.

"You have a piont, Wade. Old habits are hard to break. Did the object lesson have an effect?"

Wade Granger chuckled and downed his brandy. "Weems came around to the station house and paid up not an hour after the boys got through with him."

"Good enough, then. Which brings us to another point. Frenchy, are you sure the person you saw was Charity Rose?"

"I got two dead men to prove it," Frenchy answered bluntly.

"Yes, and one missing, along with the woman," Concho Bill countered. "I'm a bit concerned that our Miss Rose is not so dead as you think."

"So am I," Gerd Meeker injected. "My—ah— unfortunate confinement in Canyon City kept me from being involved in your earlier encounters with the young lady, but I gather she disrupted things rather effectively."

"She did," Concho Bill admitted. "When she came after us, she made us look like an unorganized mob of schoolboys. That's why I pulled in my horns and thought up this new approach to milking the suckers. You doing five years for selling a nonexistent mine hardly qualifies you as a hardened desperado, Gerd.

"But it does show you have larceny in your heart," Baudine went on flatteringly. "That, and the fact you're a damned fine mining engineer, is why I included you in this venture. I appreciate your support on this Rose matter. I'll believe she's dead when I see her body." He poured more brandy around.

Frowning, Frenchy Descoines sought to restrain the

feeling of all's well. "I'm concerned about this shake-down of the merchants. Incidents like that with Weems can be trouble for us in the long run. There's nothing keeping one of them from going to Virginia City and complaining to the U.S. marshal."

"There's nothing keeping us from blowing out some shopkeeper's brains if he tries it," Buck Harris growled. It earned him a scowl from Concho Bill.

"From here on, we'll have a new policy on that," Baudine announced. "The idea will be to squeeze tightly until they squeal, then back off a little and watch them wiggle."

Appreciative, satisfied laughter filled the room.

CHAPTER 13

Chirping brightly, the canary bobbed about in its tiny cage. Seven men gathered around it at the tunnel head on third level of the Lucky Strike mine. Their faces, all save that of Brian Killabrough, held expressions of wonder and bemusement.

" 'Tis a clever trick the Welsh miners learned from us Irish. If the wee budgie falls over dead, that means there's deadly gas in the tunnel or there isn't enough air. That's the signal to pull the pin and haul out of here, foreman or no foreman."

"Aye, lads," Conrad O'Farrel stated forcefully. "Wi'out a by your leave. No more dyin' for the mine owners because the fool foreman can't smell it any more than you."

"It's truth yer sayin', boy-o," Killabrough added. "This little bird will die of it long before you do. So there's time."

"What about the strike?" one miner asked.

"We're still up to organizin' the men, lad," Sean O'Day advised in his light tenor voice. "First that, then if

142

the management won't allow the use o' budgies, we walk out."

"I thought you come to make a strike," another complained.

"That we did, only it has to be gone about in the proper way. Make it the fault of management an' e'ryone's behind you. Just up and walk out an' ye'll find yerselves replaced overnight," Killabrough lectured.

"There's ten good men buried under that rubble in the number-two shaft. I've a good mind to have the high and mighty Mr. Holoburton pay for their lives."

"So 've I, lads," Liam Carmoody agreed with a wink. "And so he will. That, I guarantee you."

Sweetwater had grown during the five days she had been gone, Charity Rose observed. Not only had new tent-clapboard structures sprouted along the main street, but fresh houses, some still under construction, appeared along the residential avenues behind the business district. There were more women, too. Not soiled doves and dance hall tarts, but substantial women in faded print dresses, dowagers with white hair and dark, brocaded dresses. The shrill cries of children, not those compelled to work in the mines or bordellos, reached her from the yard of what appeared to be an improvised school. In her C. M. Rose garb, Charity eased Lucifer along the crowded thoroughfare to the livery stable.

"Mornin', Mr. Rose," the gnarled proprietor greeted her as Charity rode up.

"Good morning to you, Seth. Anything interesting happen while I was gone?"

"Nope. Just the usual. Drunk rowdies broke up the

general store and whupped some welts on Melvin Weems. Oh, and a prospector ran afoul of the claim-jumpers and lived to tell about it."

"He did?" Charity asked, interest growing. She might get some descriptions, something to work on. "Where is he now?"

"In that little four-bed hospital Doc Cheney put up behind his office an' apothecary. Young feller. Name of Baines, or Blount, something like—Blaine. That's it. Josh Blaine."

Charity barely controlled the beginning of a startled expression. She paled slightly and wet her lips. "I wonder if he can identify the men who jumped him?"

"Oh, he has. Told the chief all about it. Only thing, Granger ain't done a lick to arrest those responsible."

"Probably out of his jurisdiction," Charity offered.

"Not in the Bird Cage, or the Gut Bucket, or half a dozen other saloons," the hostler responded. "I think we need some new law in this town."

"I'll not argue that with you," Charity said, taking her leave.

At the small hospital, Charity found all four beds occupied. Two held miners with different work-related injuries, one contained, though barely, a spunky pre-teen lad with a faceful of freckles. Josh sat in the last, propped partially upright by a pile of pillows.

"Young man to see you, Mr. Blaine," the doctor advised as he led the way.

Midnight-blue eyes fixed on Charity and the be-speckled kid chirped brightly, "Bushwhackers shot hell outta him, mister."

Purple, green and yellow bruises around the grooved track of the bullet made Josh's head look far worse than

144

his condition allowed. Charity's lips twisted in sympathetic hurt. The spunky lad made a gun of thumb and forefinger.

"What are you in here for, son?" Charity asked.

"Mumps," he answered cheerfully. "Maw says she don't want me givin' 'em to the other kids and the doctor will make me stay in bed and that way my balls won't swell up."

"Ah, mothers," Charity said in an aside to the doctor. "What a refined, civilized influence they are."

"Heck, we're all guys in here," the boy observed incorrectly. "What difference does it make if I say balls. Maw said stones, but I knew she meant my balls."

"That's enough, Tommy," Dr. Cheney snapped. To C. M. Rose he added, "Sometimes I think Tommy has his private machinery on his brain."

"Naw. It's swingin' right between my legs where it ought to be."

"*Tommy!* Having mumps doesn't keep you from getting the razor strap on your butt," Dr. Cheney barked. "Perhaps it is a mistake to have the town grow, bring in settled people. Easterners don't have the polite manners we're accustomed to. Now, for your friend. You're looking better, Mr. Blaine," the medico called out.

"What? Uh, who are..." Recognition brought silence to Josh Blaine. Eyes wide with wonder, he blinked. "I'm sorry, I was dozing. Thank you, Doctor," he said dismissively.

After the doctor departed and the little imp, Tommy, settled in his bed, Josh spoke again. "Charity, what are... oh, I see. Your—ah—professional garb, eh?"

"Yes. I'm C. M. Rose in this getup. It's a little more convenient when I get around to capturing and turning

145

in wanted men. Josh, how did this happen?" she inquired, changing the subject.

"I got hit by claim-jumpers," Josh answered simply. "It was—oh, more than a week ago. I lay out at my claim for the better part of four days, before I could get on a horse and come to town. Lucky thing. Doc Cheney said I could have died of infection, if I didn't bleed to death first."

"Don't misunderstand me, but your head looks awful," Charity remarked.

"You ought to see my side. That's where the real damage was done. Caused me to bleed inside. They left me for dead, said they'd send someone out to take over my diggings."

"Was it really worth their killing for?"

"And how. Assayer said it graded out better than the old Comstock in Virginia City. Do you suppose it's still mine?"

Charity looked at him. "If it isn't, we'll soon make it so," she vowed. "How soon can you get out of here?"

"The doctor said today if I behaved myself."

"And have you?"

Josh produced a pink flush. "In everything but my thoughts. I could dream of nothing but hunting down those bastards and killing them ever so slowly."

"That's a weighty subject to spend all your dreams on. Didn't you have any other topics to dwell on?"

Josh's flush deepened. "Well, I—there was, I guess—you."

"Josh, I'm flattered. It's sweet of you to think of me in all your pain."

Now Josh looked chagrinned. "It—ah—wasn't—ah, well, I didn't think of you so much until I was on

146

the mend."

"And I'm still flattered." Also greatly aroused, Charity admitted privately. "Let's see the doctor about getting you out of here. Then I'm going to help you get well real fast." Impulsively, Charity bent and kissed Josh on the cheek.

"Gol-lee," Tommy croaked from behind them. "I heard about guys like you."

"Son," Charity said in a cold, grating tone. "How would you like me to hike up that nightshirt of yours and spank your bare butt?"

"No you won't," the lad taunted, then saw C. M. meant every word of it. "Maw! Maw, help me! He's gonna kill me, maw!"

She left him huddled in self-fed fright while arrangements were made for Josh to be released. Blaine dressed and departed with Charity for a couple of days in C. M. Rose's rooming house.

She stirred in the darkness. Careful not to disturb the lean, muscular man beside her, Charity Rose reached out and took the chimney from a kerosene lamp. She struck a match and held the flame to the wick, then adjusted it to provide faint, but adequate, light. Next she eagerly turned her attentions to Joshua Blaine.

Peeling back the sheet that covered him, she let her gaze rest on his chest, where a small patch of golden threads formed curls along the center line of his body. Below, his flat abdomen rose and fell in the rhythm of slumber. She let her inspection move to his pubic mound. There a coppery thatch hid the base of his semi-erect phallus. Memories of their past two nights of

147

amorous combat flooded her.

It seemed that a little good loving had been all Josh needed to complete his recovery. At least from a stamina point, Charity reflected. Eagerly she reached out to grasp his firming member and gently knead it. Josh responded at once, though still in a light doze. His manhood elongated and stiffened. With only minimal effort, Charity brought him to a full erection. Josh made soft, pleased sounds and shifted his position. Charity bent over him; her breasts and long, auburn hair brushed his belly and sent shivers through his body, awakening him as she covered the ruby bulb of his maleness with her lips.

"Ummm. Good," Josh muttered. "More. Take more of it."

Eagerly, Charity complied. Opening wide, she slid down the curved length of his throbbing shaft, tongue busy with work of its own. Josh sucked air through his teeth and trembled with delight.

"Aaaahhh, that's great," Josh sighed. He reached up and began to insinuate his hand between her thighs. Questing fingers found the sparse mat of auburn hair on her swollen cleft and parted the damp fronds to push in farther.

Charity made agreeable noises around the bulk she consumed and widened the gap between creamy thighs. She shivered mightily as Josh inserted two fingers among the leafy fronds within her portal. His manipulation rapidly warmed her to a frenzy of desire.

Swiftly she abandoned his sleek, shapely organ long enough to switch positions and lower her moist, ready cleft onto its blunt knob. She gasped as he entered her, spreading wide the constricted passage. Charity arched her back, supporting her weight against his upraised legs.

"Why the light?" Josh inquired in harsh grunts.

"I—want—to watch," Charity panted out. "I—want to—see you—moving inside me."

For long, delightful minutes, Charity pleasured them both as she skillfully brought them close to oblivion time and again. At last it could be prolonged no longer and they crashed over into the cataclysmic sensations of a splendid climax. Shuddering, her lovely breasts swayed with each paroxysm of her release. Choking sobs came from both throats as their attainment grew prolonged. At last the primal surge ebbed.

"Are we going to do anything else today?" Josh asked when reason returned.

"We're going out to your claim, if you feel up to it," Charity answered him.

"I feel more up to this," Josh teased.

"Save it for tonight," Charity suggested. "It's almost dawn."

"What a wonderful way to spend the night," Josh sighed.

"You sound like this was a first time. I know it can't be. Not the way you thrilled me."

"Then we're both happy?" Josh speculated.

"I am. Now, what would you like for breakfast?"

By eight o'clock they had been well fed and Josh admitted his concern for his rich silver strike. They left the livery stable at a quarter past ten.

Quince Ballantine considered himself lucky. First he bought an incredibly rich claim for a reasonable price, with payments monthly and a percentage. Then he had been able to hire three men with solid experience in working open-face mines. Ballantine vaguely knew of two methods of producing a yield from the type of mine he purchased.

First was the water pressure technique known as placer mining. That wouldn't do in his present situation. The other was strip-mining, the cutting away of a hillside in terraces. Fortunately his three employees knew a lot about this procedure. They had so far been taking out six to eight hundred dollars a day in startlingly rich ore. Pleased with his success so far, Quince Ballantine didn't feel the slightest unease when a scowling young man and an attractive woman rode up to his diggings.

"Good morning. Out looking for some likely prospects?" he greeted as they reined in.

"No," the man answered. "I'm interested in this mine."

"Sorry," Ballantine responded in a cheery tone. "It's definitely not for sale."

"Do you mind telling me from whom you bought it?" Josh Blaine asked.

"Why—ah—the owner, Joshua Blaine," Ballantine answered confidently.

"I'm afraid you didn't," Josh stated flatly.

"I don't understand. He put the claim up for sale in Sweetwater and I made a large downpayment. His signature is on the title."

"No, it isn't. You see, I am Joshua Blaine."

Uneasiness stole over Quince Ballantine. His normally uncomplicated mind filled with suspicions. "I don't know what you're trying to pull. I saw the abstract of the deed, the assay reports, everything. You're not trying to buffalo me out of this place, are you?"

"Not in the least. Only I do intend to heave you off my property and find the men responsible for shooting me and stealing my claim."

Charity entered the argument with a pointed question. "Would you describe this Joshua Blaine who sold you the mine?"

"I don't see why I should," Ballantine countered, growing belligerent.

"Because if you don't, we can press charges of receiving stolen property. You're occupying a claim filed by my friend here, Joshua Blaine. We can have the U.S. marshal here within three days."

"Now, see here—I—all right." Ballantine went on to describe the "Joshua Blaine" who had sold him the claim.

Filtering minor differences through her mind, Charity quickly came to the conclusion that the man Ballantine described was Concho Bill Baudine. It also came close to the man known as Victor Holoburton, whom she had not as yet seen face to face.

When Ballantine paused in his bluster, she spoke sharply to Josh.

"It's a long ride to Virginia City, Josh. We'd better be going."

"Why did you want to leave?" Josh asked, once they had ridden out of earshot.

"To give him time to stew a little. Also . . ." and she went on to tell him about the descriptions.

"Then this Holoburton is likely to be Concho Bill Baudine and used my name?"

"Exactly," Charity informed him.

Josh brushed at a stray lock of his curly, straw-yellow hair. "In which case, what do we do about it?"

"*I* hunt them down, while you get on with the business of getting well."

CHAPTER 14

Two days after their first visit to Joshua's claim, he and Charity returned. This time they brought along the assayer. This being Sunday, he had the time free for the journey. So far, Charity had not seen Holoburton to verify her suspicions. He had been out of town on business for several days. They rode up to a different kind of reception.

Quince Ballantine met them with a shotgun in hand. "I thought you were bringing the law," he challenged.

"We decided to try reasoning with you first. You know this gentleman?" Charity stated.

"Of course. That's the gover'ment's assayer. What did you bring him here for?"

"Ask him if he remembers Joshua Blaine," Charity suggested.

Ballantine did and the assayer allowed as how he did. Then he added, "He's sittin' that horse next to me."

"That can't be!" Ballantine exploded.

"I'm afraid it is," the dapper little man said primly.

"Then who sold me this mine?" Ballantine went on to

describe Concho Bill Baudine's present appearance.

"This has become quite confusing. The man you described is Victor Holoburton. He owns the Lucky Strike. Did you happen to sell this claim to him and just not remember it, Mr. Blaine?" he directed to Josh.

"I didn't sell to anyone. Claim-jumpers rode up and shot me, right over there, then took off and left me for dead."

"My—my. Someone must have bamboozled Mr. Holoburton," the assayer prattled. "I just don't understand."

"He called himself Blaine," Ballantine insisted doggedly.

"Who?" the assayer demanded.

"Blaine—er—the man who sold me the mine. Holoburton or whoever I described. Why would he do that?"

"You can't accuse Mr. Holoburton of any wrongdoing. Why, he's a pillar of the community. His mine is what holds our town together."

"Then what can I do?" Ballantine asked miserably.

"I suggest you close down your operation and move off the claim, so Mr. Blaine can have his property back. Now, my good man, don't go bellowing again," he hastily added, when Ballantine threatened to burst. "That won't get us anywhere. Perhaps you should compare the signature on your transfer deed with that of Mr. Blaine here that's in my office."

"I've been swindled; that appears sure enough. But what can I do about it?"

"Admit you made a terrible mistake and join the line of those wanting a piece of Victor Holoburton," Charity informed him. "If I'm not mistaken, his real name is Bill

153

Baudine, a hardcase from New Mexico. That being the case, you can find a place close to the gallows and wave good-bye to him after I catch up to him."

Human nature being what it is, when Ballantine departed from the claim he had bought illegally, he shared his anger equally between Concho Bill Baudine and Joshua Blaine. On the ride back into Sweetwater, Charity summed up their situation.

"All we can do is wait until this Holoburton puts in an appearance. Then, if it's Bill Baudine, I'll make my move."

"Oh, Lordie, they're killin' everyone!" a large, plain woman in faded gingham dress and bonnet cried in terror.

A steady rattle-pop of discharging firearms added credence to her claim. From the direction of the large co-op mine came the cries of agony and curses of men engaged in deadly combat. Several more of the miners' wives shouted in alarm and bustled to gather straying children.

"Hurry, hurry. We've got to help our menfolk," a younger, attractive miner's wife urged.

"We have to save the children," another added to the confusion.

Two ladies grabbed rifles, a third a shotgun. They turned to see fully half the marauders riding down on them. "Just pretend it's Indians," one of them advised the other pair.

Her advice worked well. Two men flung themselves from the saddle when the women fired their weapons. The shotgun boomed again while the two with Winchesters cycled the lever actions. A claim-jumper screamed horribly, his face torn to shreds by a load of No. 4 shot. She broke the double twelve and reloaded rapidly while her friends sent death speeding toward the killers.

"Get around them," one gunhawk advised. A moment later a shotgun load pulped his chest.

"Over there; they ain't got guns," a youthful voice broke over the words.

"Set fire to that shack," commanded a broad-shouldered outlaw with a dark smudge of five o'clock shadow.

On the slaughter went. By the time the shooting, burning and raping ended, only two women and five children had survived. An hour after the massacre, a slightly built, stooped figure stirred and sat upright.

"Grandy, help us," a woman with a broken leg called out.

"Please, Grandy, please," two small children cried.

"All right, all right, consarn it," the feisty oldster growled. "Them fellers like to broke my skull. Whooie, I'm plumb dizzy. Gimme a second, huh? Huh?"

Slowly, the nearly toothless old timer examined his aches and scrapes and came to his feet. He looked about and clasped his battered hat to his chest, wadded in a two-hand grip.

"Land of Goshen, they near kilt ever'body," he said in wonder.

A small boy of eight knelt weeping beside a golden-haired woman with a large red stain under her left breast. "Momma. Please, momma. Wake up and talk to me. I'm scared."

Fighting the tears that welled in his eyes, Hezekiah "Grandy" Spears hastened to the lad and firmly grasped

155

one shoulder. "Your momma's with the angels, boy. Now don't you cry. Be glad for her."

"B-but what about me? I saw those bad men kill my Paw. Now momma's not awake. What can I do?"

"Take hold, son, get a grip on yourself, and keep on goin', no matter."

Stricken by the pathos of the situation, Grandy Spears turned away from the boy with a helpless flutter of hands and moved along to the woman who had first called to him. He briefly examined her leg.

"Broke, all right. You'll have to see the doctor in Sweetwater for help with that."

"How do we get there?" she demanded bluntly.

"I reckon I'll have to take a horse and ride in for help," Grandy suggested.

"A lot of good that'll do," she answered bitterly. "Our menfolk murdered, women and kids, too, and those who survived violated and degraded by those monsters. No one will help us. No one cares."

"I can't say as to that, ma'am. Let me bring water to those who are in need and make all of you comfortable as possible. Then I'll go for he'p."

Clouds gathered overhead, pushing out to engulf most of the pale, blue sky. The threat of a storm, possibly even snow, forced an abrupt end to the pleasant ride in the country for Charity and Josh. They had planned to spend the entire afternoon sweeping through the varied diggings of the Sweetwater Creek area, asking questions and seeking some lead to Concho Bill Baudine or Buck Harris.

They had learned plenty, though little of immediate

156

help. When the billowing columns assembled above them, they started back for Joshua's claim. The small lodging he had put up there, made of board planks and a Sibley tent, would shelter them well enough. Charity's thoughts turned to what she would fix for their evening meal. The distant mutter of thunder competed with the rumble of dynamite blasts. Neither of them at first heard the burring growls of small animals quarreling. Charity noticed it when they came almost on top of the scene.

"Coyote pups fighting over something," she announced as she urged Lucifer closer. Then she gulped and looked away.

Two fuzzy young coyotes tugged stoutly at opposite ends of a strip of flesh. A barely human-looking carcass lay partially wrapped in a tarpaulin. Shocked momentarily, Charity recovered her aplomb, dismounted and went to examine the remains. The pups dropped their trophy, yapped their complaints and scampered away.

"It's a woman, or used to be," Charity informed Josh. "She's been dead a while. Someone just . . . dumped her here."

"What do we do?" Josh inquired. "It's a long way to the marshal in Virginia City."

"Let me think a moment." An idea swiftly grew in Charity's head. "I'm not too sure how well Frenchy bought that note I sent saying I was dead. This might be a chance to get them completely off guard."

"How do you mean?" Josh asked, viewing the corpse with distaste.

"We'll take this poor woman in to town and you claim it's me. I have a spare set of papers from Graham County and my badge. I'll put them in my buckskin pouch and you can say you found them with the body."

Josh gulped back his revulsion. "Will it work?"

"Well enough to create a lot of doubt. I'll have the advantage of surprise then. If Baudine's henchmen aren't expecting me, they won't be looking for me."

"It's a terrible thing to do."

"I know, Josh. Yet, it's a marvelous opportunity, handed to us like that," she snapped her fingers for emphasis.

Swallowing hard again, Josh agreed. He helped her prepare the impersonation and then loaded the dead woman on his nervous mount. Riding double, they returned to the camp. Charity settled down to start the cook fire, while Josh headed for town, leading the corpse on his packhorse.

Baudine's collaborating police chief was only too glad to bring a bit of good news to the Tivoli Palace for Frenchy Descoines. While he did, Josh returned quickly with the news that the identity had stuck. Disturbing thoughts kept them both more quiet than usual. Late that night, with a low wind howling outside and light rain pattering on the canvas tent, Charity came to where Josh sat, reading by the guttering light of a low-turned lantern.

"I'm sorry, Josh. I shouldn't have involved you in that terrible mess this afternoon."

"It's all right, Charity. I understand. And it's not . . . that bothering me. It's . . . Well, I got to think-ing on the way in to town. With the kind of heartless murders we have involved in this, that could as easily have been you in the tarp."

"Oh—Josh—I . . ." Charity choked on her emotion. She knelt at the side of his camp stool and wrapped her arms around his neck. Her soft, shy kisses rained down with her tears for a long while. Then, slowly, inevitably, the banked fires of passion began to glow warmer and at last burst into flame. In a terrible, overpowering frenzy they threw off their clothing and made wild, furious, ravaging love while the storm reached its crescendo and moved on.

CHAPTER 15

"It's Hez Spears," one astonished man blurted at sight of the dirty, bedraggled, blood-stained man who walked his horse into Sweetwater in late afternoon.

"Grandy, what happened?" another inquired while Spears slid from his mount's back and staggered toward the boardwalk.

"Can't you see he's hurt?" a third man chastised the curious. "Who was it, Grandy? Who did this?"

Grinding his teeth against the pain, Grandy Spears crossed the boardwalk and entered the doctor's office. From outside, the gawkers could hear the cantankerous oldster's voice as he hailed the physician.

"Hey, Doc Cheney. You've got a whole passel of folks need he'p out at the Galconda."

Speculation ran wild among the throng when Grandy lowered his volume and explained to an astonished Dr. Cheney what awaited him at the mine. The mutter of misinformation reached C. M. Rose on the fringe of the crowd.

"Don't look like he was hurt in the mine. That was a bullet hole," a more astute bystander remarked.

"Naw. They musta had a collapse out there," another stated knowingly.

"Then how come the whistle ain't blowin'?" the careful observer challenged.

"Maybe the boiler blew up."

"We'd have heard that."

C. M. Rose's husky voice entered the discussion. "What's going on?"

"Grandy Spears rode in a minute ago all dirtied up and bloody. Went to the Doc's," the reply came.

"You said he had been shot? Any idea of how or why?" C. M. pressed.

"What do you think? Claim-jumpers, I'd say."

"Thank you." C. M. pushed purposefully through the gathering and entered the doctor's office. "Mr. Spears, what happened?"

Startled, Grandy looked up at what appeared to be a young man with a pair of gooseneck Colt Bisleys strapped around his waist. "Weeel, it were them damned claim-jumpers. I was just tellin' Doc. Massacreed everyone most nearly. There's maybe half a dozen youngsters, two women and myself left. They musta thought us dead or we'd not be here."

"How long ago was this?" C. M. queried.

"Middle of the morning. They . . . hit us without warning."

"You're going back?" C. M. asked.

"Ayap. Soon's this pill-roller patches me up," Grandy assured C. M..

"Would you mind some company?"

161

"Not in the least, young feller. If you can use them decorations you're wearin', you'll be more than welcome."

In company with Joshua Blaine and Grandy Spears, Charity Rose rode to the scene of the mine massacre. Chief Granger had been there ahead of them and interviewed the survivors. Shocked by the savagery of the raid, Charity examined the ground around where most of the men had died. She went on to see where the women and children had fallen.

"Can any of you identify the men who did this?" she asked.

"Sure we can," a stout, buxom older woman declared. "We described them to the chief. We'll have a hard time proving it, what with all the men dead, but one of ours yelled that it was Buck Harris and his gang a while before th-they killed him."

"You told the sheriff that?"

"Yep. He seemed not to believe it," the woman told Charity.

"More'n that, maw," a skinny, stringy boy with the same soft features and fine, fair hair injected. "Chief Granger acted as if he didn't really care what happened to us and wouldn't do anything about it."

"Peter," the woman snapped. "You mind what you say."

"It's true, maw. It was like all the time he was laughing at us. Or disappointed we had lived through it. Everybody knows the chief is in Mr. Holoburton's pocket."

"That's enough, son. What possible reason would Mr.

162

Holoburton have for not wanting us to work our mine? He has the Lucky Strike."

Images of a smirking Concho Bill Baudine rose in Charity's mind. "I think the boy may have something. We'll establish their trail and follow for most of the day. Then I think I'll pay a call on the chief of police."

Despite her ordeal, the miner's widow managed to glance dubiously sideways at Charity. "What's your interest in all this, mister?"

C. M. Rose sighed and put one hand on the grip of a Colt Bisley. "I don't like seeing innocent people hurt. And there are bound to be some rewards on the animals who did this. I'm a bounty hunter, and I intend to collect on those."

"More power to you," the gritty widow declared.

"Mr. Rose, I have a hanker to go along with you," Grandy Spears announced as he walked up. "That wound's just a scratch, don't pain me at all anymore."

"I want to go, too," Peter piped.

"Peter!" his shocked mother rapped out. "You're not going anywhere; you're just a small boy."

"I'm twelve," Peter said in hot defense of his offer.

"That's what I said—a little boy," his mother ended the subject.

Peter shoved out his pink underlip in a schoolboy pout. Charity put a hand on the boy's shoulder and shook him gently. "Maybe next time, Peter."

"Won't be no next time."

"What about me? Nobody's said if I go or not," Grandy complained irrascibly.

"You can come if you want, Grandy. Take it easy on your wound, though."

"Oh, I will. That I will."

"So, the first thing is to cut sign of their trail at some distance from here, figure out how many there are. Then we hunt them down and make them into gallows fruit."

Finding the trail and marking it took little time. It soon became obvious why the Harris gang had evaded capture for so long. The general direction of the multiple trails, after a dispersion some three miles from the scene of the massacre, led westward toward the Sierra Nevada. Joshua and the rest continued on the clearest of these while Charity rode back to Sweetwater.

Still in her C. M. Rose garb, she paid a call on the chief of police. At first glance he appeared to be a man capable of his office. Charity judged him to be in his mid to late forties. He had started to put on a bit of belly behind his gunbelt. The milky, disfigured iris of one eye gave him a disconcerting walleyed expression. She told him the purpose of her visit and his response surprised her.

"Oh, that," Chief Granger prefaced his response. "It just happened and already people are complaining, eh?"

"According to the witnesses, the Harris gang was involved. Have you put out reward posters on them as yet?" Charity probed.

"Nope. Who'd pay if anybody brought them in? Not for that bunch."

Charity had so far found Chief Granger much as the boy had described. His continued indifference goaded her. "Men, women and children have been murdered, some of the women violated. Surely there's enough community outrage to obtain donations for a reward."

"Don't see why. Those folks were squatters—on the place illegally. The mine, according to the latest listings at the claims office, belongs to Mr. Victor Holoburton."

"I keep hearing that name. What's Mr. Holoburton like?" Charity asked.

"A man with a lot of influence. Rich. Don't show himself around town much. Keeps to himself and don't stick his nose in, like some people I could name." Granger coldly eyed C. M. Rose. "He's tall, black hair . . ." Wade Granger went on to describe Concho Bill Baudine, except for the mustache, longer hair and gaudy clothes. "No, I think you'll find little sympathy for those folks around this town."

"I wonder how they'll see it in Virginia City?"

"Go if you want; it's a fool's errand," Granger said confidently.

In the enlarged camp at Joshua's mining claim, Charity informed her companions of Granger's attitude. Grandy Spears wasted no time in expressing his opinion.

"Never did trust that mother's son. Him going all the time to those meetings with Descoines of the Tivoli Palace and Holoburton from the Lucky Strike. Ask me, they had him in their hip pockets."

"What's that? What meetings?" Charity prodded.

"Why, every week or so they all gather at that flashy brothel and have a fancy dinner, lots to drink, and our fine chief of police is right there with the rest."

Charity told of her conviction that Holoburton was Baudine. That brought a response from Grandy. "Heard of that Baudine feller from down Colorado way. He ran a gang in New Mexico, right? They knocked over a big gold shipment outside Durango while I was minin' there."

"That's the one," Charity told him.

"Well, then, C. M., we better make some plans on how to deal with that one. If he's in with Buck Harris we're facin' a whole lot of trouble."

"I think he's more than *in* with Harris, I think he gives the orders."

"If that's the case, how can we make him show his hand?" Grandy asked.

"I consider the best way is to take back some of what he's stolen."

"Such as, C. M.?" Grandy asked.

"We've already recovered Josh's claim. Signatures in the land title office took care of that. We need something else, equally big."

Grandy brightened. "How about the Lucky Strike? It belonged to a friend of mine. I'll swear he was cheated out of it in a crooked card game at that confounded Tivoli Palace. Next thing anyone knows this Victor Holoburton comes to town and he's the owner."

Charity produced a frown. "It would be hard for only three people to seize something that big."

Disappointment showed on Grandy's face. "Wull, there's the Five Hearts. Three fellers I prospected with had that. Two of them wound up dead, and the last one is supposed to have wandered off drunk one night and disappeared. But I know where he is. Could have him back here in a day or two. Since he left, the mine's had a whole passel of owners, but right now it's back in Holoburton's hands. I'll lay every ounce of silver I ever earn that he's behind that, too."

"Fine. Where is it?" Charity asked.

Quickly Grandy described the ill-fortuned mine. Charity asked a few questions. Josh contributed that he had some dynamite on hand if it would help. By then

166

Charity had a plan in her head.

"We'll get that mine back from Holoburton all right. And we'll take his next silver shipment. We'll do it by using the same tactics Baudine's henchmen employ."

Guarding this damn-fool place had always been a bust. No one was going to come around shooting up the place. Not when it belonged to Victor Holoburton. Not when the guards were, as far as they knew, members of the only gang jumping claims in the Sweetwater area. A tall fence of barbed wire and hog enclosure, supported by fifty stout aspen poles, now covered the front of the operation. A big double gate allowed ore wagons in and out. Usually both guards slept through the night. This night one remained awake, if not alert, with a stomach troubled by some too-old pork.

He spent most of his time in, or on his way to or from, the small outhouse that had been built to one side, some twenty yards inside the fence. The first Harry York knew about trouble was when the inside of the shack washed a bright white, which quickly faded to a dull red-orange where the gates should have been. When the sound of the blast ravaged his ears, and the shock wave reached the chicksale. The jolt knocked the small structure over before Harry had his trousers up.

He sprawled upside down in the overturned convenience, and for a moment knew real horror when he believed he would slide backward into the foul pit underneath. He clawed frantically at the door, which occupied the place the bare rafters should have been. The outhouse rocked dangerously, and he shrank back in fear of dislodging the whole mess. Sandy ground grated under the structure and brought a new burst of energy from Harry.

With a mighty shove, he succeeded in throwing the door up and over. He saw pinpoint stars in the velvet blackness above him. Then he vaulted over the lip onto secure ground. To his right he saw that his partner had been jolted out of a deep sleep. Not more than a few seconds could have gone by, Harry judged. Who could have done a thing like that?

In the pale moonlight, Harry saw that one gate remained upright, canted askew from its lower hinge, a huge crescent hole blown out of the inner edge. He saw no one, no attackers, so he knew it only seemed as if it had taken hours to get out of the shithouse. He heard a sharp grating sound behind him and half turned to see the outhouse slide into the refuse pit below. Christ, he could have been in there. His rifle still was.

Harry pulled up his trousers and drew his sixgun. Crouched low, he called to his partner in a harsh shout, "Charlie, you all right?"

"Yeah. What about you?"

"Damned near went in the shitter. What happened?"

"Someone dynamited the gate—what do you think?" Charlie responded.

"Where are they?"

Charity Rose and her two companions answered all his questions then by thundering through the shattered gates at a full gallop.

Bent low over Lucifer's outstretched neck, Charity rode toward the crouched figure of the guard near the defunct outhouse. Hours of stern self-discipline and tedious practice had honed her ability to shoot and hit on the run. The Bisley in her right hand belched yellow-orange flame and her target tumbled to one side. To her right, Josh and Grandy charged the other, less vulnerable sentry. Twenty-five miners, working the late shift, remained inside the earth, at the tunnel head. Faintly they heard the reports of firearms and wanted nothing to do with that. Charity swung away when she had made sure the first guard was out of action.

"I'm going to the mine," she shouted to Josh. "We'll have to get the miners out of there."

A bullet cracked past her head and she fired reflexively. The heavy .45 slug struck a boulder and sent a shower of granite slivers into Charlie's eyes. Howling in pain, blinded by powdered stone, he staggered into the open. He held one hand to his face, the other high in the air. Charity reined in.

"He can be of use to us," she stated, preventing Grandy from gunning down the helpless man. "The men underground know his voice. We'll let him call them out."

"Then what?" Charlie asked in a surly tone.

"We blow the tunnel. This mine is going back to its rightful owner. He'll have some work to do," Charity added, "but I don't think he'll mind."

Within twenty minutes the miners had come to the surface and started on the long road to Sweetwater. Charlie hobbled along with them, without boots or belt. Charity noted the slope to his shoulders, and his hanging head.

"I have a feeling he'll keep on walking right out of the

area. Baudine has little patience with men who fail him."
She paused and looked around. "Well, what do we do next?"

"How about a nice big labor strike to tie up income from the Lucky Strike?" Grandy asked.

"That's not something we can arrange overnight," Charity protested.

"Ayap. I've heard rumors, though, that a number of fellers have come here lately from back East. Union organizer types. Now mind you, I ain't privy to what they have in mind, but my guess is they are already working on a strike."

Encouraged, Charity brightened. "Do you know them, Grandy?" At his nod, she went on, "What say we pay them a little visit?"

CHAPTER 16

Coal and wood smoke hung in wreaths over Sweetwater, staining the pink and pale blue of sunrise with gray streaks. Grandy Spears and his friend showed up at the land office ahead of any other eager claimants. When the fussy clerk—a political appointee of the territorial governor—arrived, he made them wait on the chilly stoop while he went inside, relocking the door behind him. He lighted the potbellied stove, set coffee to brewing, raised the blinds and opened his ledger. Only then did he unlock the door and admit them.

"Rupe here's bought his claim back from Holoburton," Grandy announced.

He, too, knew Cassius Varney the forger. Grandy also knew a few things about Varney that convinced the talented scribe to restore the title to its previous, legal owner.

"I come to register the deed," Rupe added.

"I trust everything is in proper order," the pursemouthed clerk clucked primly.

" 'Course it is," Grandy assured him. "I was a witness.

171

M'signature's right there. Now get on with it."

"Do you have the filing fee?"

"Hell, no," Grandy snapped as he shelled out a twenty-dollar gold piece. "Never took a thing like that into consideration."

"Official transactions have no room for levity, Mr. Spears," the prissy bureaucrat chided.

"He-he, now ain't he screwed down right tight, Rupe? Maybe if we had some of his spirit in official transactions people wouldn't have such a pucker on their bungholes."

"Your vulgarity is offensive, if only predictable," the clerk huffed.

"Never mind that. Jist put down the facts and figgers in that ledger."

Eyes rolled toward the ceiling in supplication, the land clerk sighed wearily. "We all have our crosses to bear."

"Right enough, an' Rupe wants to start bearin' his out at his claim," Grandy snapped.

"I've a feeling something unpleasant will come of this."

Grandy's face became crimson as he glowered at the clerk. "It sure will if you don't stop flappin' yer jaw." When the clerk started to note the details of the transfer, Grandy turned to slap Rupe on one shoulder. "That's only the start, Rupe. We've got a lot more to do."

His rage could have turned the air blue. "Goddamnit, I tell you that Charity Rose is behind this," Concho Bill Baudine roared. "The law don't work this way and who else would dare go after us so viciously?"

"She's dead, Bill," Frenchy Descoines said soothingly. "I saw her body when it was brought in."

172

"You made a mistake, Frenchy," Bill returned, calming somewhat.

"Well, what I saw had red hair, but the—ah—animals hadn't left a lot to recognize. I took the doctor's word and Granger's."

"Neither of whom had ever seen Charity Rose."

"Not so. The doctor said he had treated her for a minor flesh wound when she first came here."

"How far can we trust Cheney? We don't own him," Bill reminded his partner.

"Rumor has it," Gerd Meeker injected, "that a young bounty hunter, named C. M. Rose, is behind the destruction of the Five Hearts. It was also him and a friend who brought in Charity's body. Saaay . . . They both have the same last name."

"Of course they do," Concho Bill snapped. "C. M. Rose is Charity Moira Rose." To Buck Harris he commanded, "Get that stupid bastard Granger over here. I want him to arrest C. M. Rose, and then we'll be rid of her for damn sure."

"Chief Granger told me to give you this," the button-nosed kid with an unruly mop of black hair and obsidian eyes chirped at C. M. Rose as he handed over a folded paper.

"Thank you," Charity rustle-voiced. She gave the boy a dime.

"Gosh. Thanks, mister." He scurried away with visions of horehound drops and rock candy in his head.

"It says," Charity informed Joshua, "that the chief now has wanted posters on the claim-jumpers. A 'committee of responsible businessmen' has put up the

173

money. I'm to come and get them right away."

"And you don't suspect something?" Joshua probed.

"If I'm right, he'd made a sidewinder look straight. That's why you're coming along with me."

"Hmmm. I thought you preferred to work alone."

"I do. But no one walks into a lion's cage with only a whip and a chair."

Five minutes later, at the police station, Chief Granger came from his office with three officers in tow. The trio spread out as Granger made his intentions known.

"C. M. Rose, Charity Rose, whatever you call yourself, I'm arresting you for the murder of an unknown young woman, whose corpse Blaine brought in here."

"Like hell you are," Joshua barked. "I'm the one who found that body. You can't get away with something like this."

"I'd say I already have," Granger said with a nod.

A nightstick swished through the air and struck a musical bong off Josh's head. He dropped to the floor without another sound.

"Book him for resisting arrest. Disarm them and get them both into cells."

"You do work for Baudine, don't you."

"Who's Baudine?" Granger asked coolly. "Get 'em out of here."

Two policemen disarmed Charity and took her by the arms. They roughly hustled her into the corridor of the cellblock and stopped outside an empty cell. One of them gestured to her man's shirt and trousers.

"Take 'em off."

"I'll not," Charity snapped.

"You will . . . or we will."

"Then you'd better get at it," Charity snarled as she

put all her weight behind her right shoulder and launched the heel of her right hand at the nearest policeman's jaw.

His head snapped to one side at the impact and something made a dull popping sound. Howling in pain, he clapped a hand to his jaw. "She bwoke it. Ga'damn she bwoke my zaaw."

Charity had continued her motion and followed through with a solid kick to the injured officer's crotch. Robbed of his breath, his gonads on fire, eyes bugged and mouth forming an agonized "O," he dropped to his knees. His partner swung his wicked oak billy a fraction of a second later.

With a quick duck and side-step, Charity avoided the murderous stick and drove two fists into the over-balanced policeman's gut. Her light weight and small frame did little damage against a powerfully built man, yet it served to distract him long enough for her to slam his arm backward against the jamb of the open cell door. A dry-stick crack and his scream of agony told her she had succeeded in breaking his nightstick arm. Quickly she snatched up the keys and started for the door at the far end of the corridor.

"Take us along!"

"Open the door," called prisoners who had observed the sudden change in events.

"Let me out!"

Charity reached her goal and started to fumble through keys, trying to open the big lock in a heavy, outside door. Behind her the officer with the broken arm had recovered himself enough to lumber after her. She fought incipient panic that threatened to spill over and render her efforts useless. Big, flat feet pounded the

175

flagstone floor of the cellblock. Suppressing a sob of desperation, Charity found the right key. Before she could insert it, the door at the office end of the corridor slammed open.

Mind fogged with pain and retreating unconsciousness, Joshua Blaine stumbled when one policeman gave him a vicious shove between the shoulder blades that propelled him into the cellblock. His captors entered behind him and shut off that hope of escape with a loud bang and the scrape of a lock. Joshua paused and took stock when he heard the startled exclamations of the two officers.

"What the hell?"

"Jeez, Jake, what happened?"

Jake sat in the middle of the corridor, one hand clasped to his crotch, the other holding his jaw. Beyond him, Josh saw imperfectly that Charity struggled with another policeman at the far end of the cellblock. Now, his mind demanded, strike while they're distracted.

Numbed by the force of the earlier blow, his body would not obey him. It seemed to take a month to ball his fists, longer to raise one arm and start a hefty roundhouse swing. Almost in a blur, it seemed, his would-be victim raised an arm to block. Joshua tried a short jab at his opponent's unprotected chin. Pain radiated up from his knuckles when the fist contacted the wrong spot.

Agony drove the last wisps of dullness from his brain. With a quick grab he wrested the nightstick from his stunned victim and smashed it down on the policeman's head. Josh sent a lashing kick at the surprised cop's midsection and broke his arm at the wrist with a powerful blow from the billy club.

Howling in anguish, the battered officer stumbled backward. Joshua took time to strike the badge-toter again, then advanced with a backswing aimed at the retreating lawman's head. A loud click and forceful bellow behind him arrested Joshua's further violence.

"That's about enough! Hold it, or I'll blow you in half," Chief Granger roared from the open doorway.

Two more clicks sounded and the chief felt a pair of cold, cold rings of steel against the back of his neck, at the base of his skull. "You got the right of that, Chief," Grandy Spears said from behind the sawed-off L. C. Smith 10-gauge. "Take your finger off that trigger or I'll lift your head offen your shoulders. Now, real slow, lower that rifle and lean it against the cell to your left." He raised his voice and hollered down the cellblock. "Feller, if you don't want to be wearin' the chief's brains for a neck scarf, let go that young lady and step to the side. Go he'p her, Josh."

Gaping at the unexpected reinforcement, Josh stumbled along past the cells to the far end. There he shoved the officer in question into an empty cell and took the keys from Charity. With a deft turn, he secured the helpless lawman.

"We'll do the rest of them the same way and then get out of here," he directed.

"I—thank you, Josh. I don't think I could have managed without you," Charity panted out.

"You seemed to be doing all right when I got here," Josh said lightly.

"And you, Granger," Charity called out as they advanced along the corridor. "How did you happen to be here?"

"When we got done at the land office, I heared that

177

you had been asked to the stationhouse. With all that's goin' on, I didn't think that could lead to nothin' good, so I come along right quick."

"Glad you did," Charity stated honestly. "Let's get the rest of them in cells. I—I suppose this makes me a fugitive?"

"Us, Charity," Joshua corrected. "Me because I'm going with you and Grandy for jailbreak."

"Then we'd better hurry. There's still one policeman out there."

"Yeah," Joshua acknowledged. "Sergeant Bleaker."

"By the time he finds out, we'll be long gone," Charity assured her companions.

A cascade of golden leaves swirled around Charity Rose as she reined in at the edge of a stand of aspens. Joshua Blaine and Grandy Spears joined her. The old man had what it took, Charity had to admit. He hadn't slowed them down and showed no sign of strain from the hard ride.

"Why'd we come clear up here?" Grandy asked. "We're a long way from Sweetwater."

"I figured the one place they would never look is close to Buck Harris's hideout. We tracked some of Harris' men this far before, so the Sierra Nevada seem a safe place."

"That's good thinkin'," Grandy allowed. "Where we headed now?"

"Some place with water and shelter, good graze, and where we can watch all the trails into the Sierra," Charity listed.

"Ummmm. Don't ask for much, do you?"

"Why, you old far— Grandy, you're making fun,

aren't you?" Charity reacted.

"Hmmmm. Won't say that I am, won't say that I ain't. You been doin' a good job leadin' so far. Keep it up."

Charity found what they wanted within two hours. For the next three days the fugitives watched every trail into the Sierra, until satisfied no pursuit had been taken this far. The nights became a torment for Charity. In recurring dreams she lived what might have happened had she not been able to escape the hands of Granger's minions. Memories of the terrible afternoon when she had seen her father murdered and endured the brutal sexual assault of Concho Bill Baudine's gang haunted her. She grew moody and snappish. At last, their supplies running low, she decided that they had to take the risk of letting Grandy ride into Virginia City for coffee, flour, beans and bacon.

After he departed, Charity sat down with Joshua and explained her nighttime demons. Josh listened in stunned reaction to the idea of such a disaster befalling anyone as lovely and vivacious as Charity. He refrained from interrupting, intimidated by the pain in her expression. When she came to the end of her tale, and summarized by saying her experience had motivated her search for revenge, Josh at last asked a question.

"Through all of that, not even once, didn't you ever think of just giving up?"

"How could I? My father had been murdered, I had been despoiled by seven dirty, unshaven, animal-minded men, Baudine was free and still menaced honest people. What was I to do?"

"But to hunt them down yourself, to bring them to justice, or to k-kill them . . . it seems an impossible task."

"Believe me, Josh, I thought so too. Often. Then,

179

when I found I could talk about it without withdrawing into a shell, or bursting out in hysterical tears, I knew I could whip anything. I trained, worked so hard every day, to learn to use a gun, a knife, a rope, how to survive in the desert, how to track someone. All for the time when I could make Baudine pay. And he did. In the first year I started tracking the gang, I killed seven men. I put five more in jail and two of those wound up on the gallows."

Joshua reached out to her, but she gently pushed his arm away. "And I felt good, Josh. I felt better than I had since before that day. I felt cleaner, like a part of the filth they had heaped on me had been scraped smoothly away. Every time I trip the trigger on one of Baudine's scum, the mocking sound grows a little bit dimmer. Someday I won't hear it any longer."

"Then will you quit?" Joshua asked in a sympathetic tone.

"Yes—when I get to piss on the grave of Concho Bill Baudine."

"Is vengeance all that drives you?"

"No, Josh, it's not. I've found that I like what I do for a living. It pays better than anything else a woman can do. I'm good at it. I'm not ready for marriage, a house with white picket fence and kiddies running around."

"You're punishing yourself, Charity," Josh blurted.

"You sound like my Aunt Megan Glendennon, my mother's sister. It's the kind of life I've chosen—hunting men. Not just Baudine's gang, either. Anyone with a price on his head."

CHAPTER 17

Only a twister could have moved through Virginia City faster than the twenty-five men who charged into town to rob the two large banks and carry off saddlebags stuffed with ingots from the silver depository. They worked in near silence, terse orders snapped to the unfortunate employees of the three establishments.

"Keep 'em up," growled a masked bandit.

"You, teller, empty your till into this bag," another snarled.

"Nobody move and you won't get hurt," a third promised.

"Hurry up! Hurry up!" a somewhat pudgy outlaw snapped at the clerks in the depository.

From the outside, life seemed to go on as usual. A few more loungers than ordinary filled benches or leaned against tie-rails, a lot of horses occupied space side-by-side, and big-eyed youngsters were urged to go play elsewhere. Nothing unusual for a busy Monday morning. Then the first shot cracked from the Comstock Traders Bank.

181

A woman's scream followed as the slug punched a hole in the belly of a plump vice-president who compounded folly by going for a gun in his desk drawer. At once the constabulary of the city converged on the center of the business district. The first two to arrive attracted the second and third shots, and fell wounded from the bullets those discharges propelled. Small boys shrilled with delight and dodged behind the dubious protection of water barrels and crated goods awaiting movement into various shops. Horses snorted and reared. The door to the Comstock Traders Bank flew open and two men in dingy, grayed linen dusters rushed out, followed by three more. They carried bountifully filled canvas bags of coin and paper currency.

Halfway down the block, the same thing happened at the Territorial Trust Bank. There no weapons had as yet been fired. The last man to leave backed out, his weaving sixgun covering the thoroughly cowed patrons and employees. One guard, not so intimidated as the others, snatched up a short-barreled shotgun and splashed bits of flannel shirt, flesh and blood on the etched, beveled glass panels of the double doors with a load of zero-zero buckshot that ripped the life from the overconfident robber.

"Damn, they got Joe," one bandit declared as he swung into the saddle.

"No time to get even," the masked hardcase beside him reminded. "Remember the orders."

"Sure, sure. Scoop the money and run. I say we shoot up the town anyway. Keep people's heads down and let us build up a little headway."

"Nothing wrong with that," his friend assured him.

At the depository, ten pair of saddlebags bulged with

silver ingots. Borne by two men each, they added two-hundred-pound handicaps to the unfortunate horses designated to haul them. Bound and gagged, the manager and three clerks looked on helplessly while the thieves departed with whoops of elation. Their sudden appearance behind the local lawmen created pandemonium.

Caught between a cross-fire, front and rear, the constabulary fled for cover within the buildings to each side. The Harris gang thundered down the street and out of town, firing random shots into building fronts and windows with an abandon unrivaled by the most pent-up trail crew hitting Dodge city.

"We gonna round up a posse?" one constable asked the town marshal.

"Not my jurisdiction. Though I suppose . . . hot pursuit and all that. I'll check with Marshal Donovan."

Within twenty minutes a unwieldy posse of thirty men set out after the outlaws. The trail led toward the Sierra Nevada. Out ahead of the posse, and only slightly behind the robbers, Grandy Spears made his way toward the camp of his friends. He reckoned correctly that the news of the robbery would be important to Charity Rose. He noted carefully where the first pair of riders broke off from the gang. Half a mile along three more diverged from the main road.

By the time Grandy reached his own diversion point, not a single outlaw remained on the trail ahead. With care, Grandy wiped out his tracks for enough distance to insure he didn't lead the posse to their fugitive encampment. From a vantage point he watched the posse rumble on by, reduced now to fifteen who followed an empty trace.

183

"Ayap," Grandy said aloud to his horse, "I reckon the others will get themselves lost, wander around a while and then head home. Them boys have a right smart tactic. No wonder they haven't been caught."

When he reached the small canyon where Charity and Joshua waited, he quickly gave them the news. Charity brightened immediately. "We know where they usually join up again. Chances are we can get there before most of them and follow Buck Harris's gang back to their hideout."

"But they always wipe out their tracks," Grandy observed.

"Which only works if no one is watching while they do it," Charity stated. "I intend to have us in position to follow no matter what they do."

Half an hour later Charity eased into a hollow in the ground from which point she could see the seven outlaws waiting in a copse of fir trees. Three more longriders approached, reining in at a hundred yards. One rose in his stirrups and whistled. A reply came a moment later. Nodding in satisfaction, the trio rode into the evergreens. Charity signaled to Joshua and Grandy and settled in to wait.

Time inched by over three hours as more of the bandits gathered. A group of twelve set out, one man walking behind, brushing out tracks. When seven more joined those in the stand of conifers, a group of nine departed. The sun slanted long down the western bowl of sky by the time the last of the outlaws reached the rally point. They set off immediately. Charity waved her companions to join her.

"That makes twenty-four, like you said, Grandy," she declared. "Now we follow along to their hideout."

"They're heading into high country," Joshua observed.

"All the better," Charity remarked. "That reduces the number of options they have."

"How do we keep with them and not be seen?' Joshua asked.

"For all their precautions, the grass won't be settled or broken ground dried out for a good fifteen minutes after they pass a given point. All we need to do is watch for bent stems and dark spots where hoofprints have been broken up. For us the trail will be as fresh as if they had done nothing."

"You didn't learn all that in Mrs. Abbott's School for Refined Young Women," Grandy observed.

"That's for sure," Charity agreed with a laugh. "My father had me tracking animals at seven and hunting them at eight. I learned more from the children of some friendly Navajo who lived not far from Dos Cabezas."

"Well, I—I guess you couldn't get better teachers," Josh responded lamely. "When do we start?"

"Now," Charity informed them.

Long bars of twilight color painted the sky when Charity and her companions came upon the hidden camp of the Harris gang. The high, steep walls of the box canyon provided excellent concealment for the hardcases, even allowing for smoke to dissipate before rising high enough to be seen from a distance. The stronghold consisted of two log cabins and a small, low barn. Most of the men slept in the warren of tents arranged haphazardly around the permanent structures. Charity wondered if the wood and dry hay would produce a thick

185

enough column of smoke to mark the obscure lair.

Before the night was over, she intended to find out, she informed Joshua and Grandy. Meanwhile a wild celebration went on and all they could do was wait. Bonfires glowed brightly, while men laughed and talked and roved around the encampment flourishing whiskey bottles, eating from a dozen cooking fires where venison and beef roasted on spits. Someone broke out a guitar and began to chord a familiar tune. Rough male voices joined in.

Half a dozen slatternly women shrieked like magpies and made their way through the lounging outlaws, dispensing their favors in liberal fashion. Two of the drabs coupled with their chosen men in the open, to the raucous advice of the onlookers. When the grunting and panting ended, they picked themselves up and went in search of new partners.

"Goddamn, woman, you're dry as a corn cob," the nearest of the fornicators complained, as he thrust himself into a blowsy harlot.

"Get on with your pokin'; there's others waitin' for some fun."

Around two in the morning, the outlaws' drunkenness reached the blind staggers stage. Many had already crawled away to sleep it off, or passed out in circles around the fires. Silently, Charity and her friends moved into position to attack the camp. One inebriated hardcase roused and staggered off from the firelight to relieve himself. He cursed softly in the night as he fumbled with the buttons of his fly.

With one hand occupied holding his limp member, he let fly a golden stream. Sudden sharp violence ended his call of nature when a slender knife blade slid into his back and sliced through his right kidney. A hand over the wounded outlaw's mouth, Grandy pulled his Greenriver blade free and shoved again, obliterating the left kidney. His victim shivered and convulsed and the old-timer lowered the corpse to the ground.

Heads muzzy with drink, Buck Harris and his gang awakened to the heavy boom of a .56 Sharps buffalo gun. The clatter of pounding hoofs across the rocky shelves of the creek brought them more bad news. From long range, Grandy provided covering fire with the Sharps while Charity and Joshua galloped into the confused camp, blasting to left and right.

Befuddled hardcases scattered like quail. Two rose from their drunken slumber to offer resistance. Charity put a .45 slug in the heart of one man and Joshua downed the other with a belly wound. Shrieking like a madman, Buck Harris attempted to rally some sort of defense. The sorrowful sluts of the previous night's bacchanalia wailed in terror and added their own blind flight to the turmoil. Charity's Bisley blazed again and again as she streaked for the squat barn. On the way she bent low and snatched up a firebrand with her free hand. A resolute defender appeared in the doorway with a rifle.

He never fired it. Charity heaved the burning billet at him and followed it with 255 grains of lead from the .45 Bisley. Bouncing beyond the fallen man, the flaming brand ignited loose hay and spread rapidly into the barn. In seconds the structure became engulfed in a roaring conflagration. Charity's keen hearing recorded a change in their supporting fire. Grandy had exhausted his Sharps ammunition and moved in closer to use his 10-gauge L. C. Smith.

Grandy's shot columns brought howls of anguish from men struck with random pellets. Buckshot slashed through the walls of tents, downing men who struggled to slide into boots and gunbelts. Joshua indicated he had reached his pre-selected goal with a gout of flame from the gang's storehouse. Curses and bellows of rage answered his deed. Charity gunned down two more men, whose wounds deprived them of their stoic demeanor.

One cried like a baby and called for his mother, while the other groaned and whimpered and crawled toward the bass bellow of Buck Harris's voice. Charity reached the corral and flung off the rope loop that secured the gate. She wedged Lucifer inside and quickly set the horses to a neck-stretching run out into the maelstrom of the camp. Beyond the corral, the horses put out for grazing jumped into a stampede at the shouts and gunshots provided by Joshua Blaine. Less than two minutes had passed since the start of the raid and Charity was on the way to fire Harris's headquarters building.

Three men leaped up to stop her. Lucifer reared and struck out with his forehoofs like a war horse. With a wailing cry, his skull crushed by an iron-shod hoof, one outlaw fell away. Charity held on and settled her powerful gelding. She slashed downward with the heavy barrel of her Bisley and felt bone give in the top of another hardcase's head. The third tottered away backward, hands lifted in supplication. The way to the log cabin lay open.

Charity swung into a skidding dismount and touched a flickering match to the short fuse that ran to a cap in a three-stick bundle of dynamite. When the black string sputtered and smoked, she hurled it through a small window and vaulted back aboard Lucifer. Churning muscles in the big black's haunches carried her safely away before the blast went off, hurling Buck Harris to the ground. Firing behind them, Charity, Joshua, and Grandy rode off into the night.

Face stained with dirt, Buck Harris came to his feet and shook impotent fists at the departing raiders. "Goddamn you—GODDAMN YOU!" Harris screamed after them. Swearing evilly, he turned aside to begin the task of assessing the damages.

Late the following afternoon, Frenchy Descoines visited the offices of Mr. Victor Holoburton. His grim expression prepared Concho Bill Baudine in part for the news he brought.

"We got trouble. Buck Harris sent in a rider a little while ago. Seems his stronghold out in the Sierra isn't so strong after all. A gang of men attacked last night and burned all the buildings, ran off a lot of livestock and shot hell out of his men. A dozen or so are talking about pulling stakes."

"Charity Rose. It had to be her, damnit."

"This is one son-of-a-bitch setback, Bill," Frenchy tried to impress on his partner.

"And one vicious bitch who has caused it. We have to stop her now, Frenchy. I mean right now."

Descoines produced a rueful smile. "First we have to find her, *mon ami.* So far it seems she is better at finding us than the other way around."

"I've been working on it. I think I have come up with a means for drawing her out, getting her right where we want her, and finishing it in a hail of lead."

"*Tres bien.* What is it?"

Grinning away his momentary outburst of rage, Concho Bill Baudine swiftly began to lay out his scheme for a deadly trap.

CHAPTER 18

For a few days, peace returned to the long valley south of Virginia City. Before the clever plot could be put into effect, all the Baudine men, and those Harris guns not involved in the Virginia City holdups and resultant raid, had to be rounded up and their leaders given their role. The least obvious place for such a gathering was the Tivoli Palace. Fifteen hard-faced gunhawks met with Concho Bill and Frenchy in a large, private dining room on the ground floor. While they gathered, the presence of so many hardcases attracted the attention of Della Terrace. When repeated mention of C. M. and Charity Rose drifted out of the crowded room, she put herself in a better position to overhear.

"You men get this straight. No one is to open fire until I do," Concho Bill demanded. "We draw her into that narrow defile south of the Virginia City road and blast her to doll rags."

"How are you gonna get her there, boss?" a ruddy-faced individual asked.

"That is being taken care of by others. I know Charity

rather well after all this time. She's one of these persons who can't stand to see a bird with a broken wing and not do something to help it. The only way to separate her from the two riding with her is to bring a world of hurt to someone she cares about. Then she'll do what she's told. And at that point, we spring the trap."

"Who around her qualifies for that condition?" Chief Granger inquired.

Della worked her way along the veranda, closer to the open window, eager to hear every word. For a moment the dark curve of her long hair extended beyond the sash. In that fraction of time Frenchy Descoines looked up and saw the swift disappearance as Della Terrace jerked her head back. The eye-blink impression had been so fleeting he discounted its relevance. He returned his attention to the meeting.

"For a while I couldn't come up with anyone," Concho Bill admitted. "Then I recalled that rooming house where she stayed as C. M. Rose. She and the woman who ran it got to be quite friendly. So a couple of the boys have gone over to get Mrs. Foster and entertain her in some safe place. A lock of her hair and a tear-stained note ought to bring our dear Rose out in the open quickly enough."

Agitated by this news, Della debated waiting longer or doing something immediately to warn Charity. She had promised Della help in getting away from the Tivoli Palace, and Della felt a kinship with the strange, bounty-hunting young woman. She remained at her post only long enough to hear again the location of the planned trap. Then she hurried away to her room. Twenty minutes later, Wesley, the young towel-boy for the establishment, answered a summons from Della. Quickly she explained what she wanted and sent the lad on his way.

Concho Bill Baudine saw the distant flash of light, the signal that Charity Rose had taken the turn that would bring her into the trap. He clapped his hands together and rubbed them in eager anticipation. So far everything had gone well.

Two of his men had taken Amanda Foster to a remote mining claim to hold until Charity Rose had been killed. The rest of the gang, including Baudine, had ridden to the selected spot and set up their ambush. Only minutes remained before Baudine would achieve his long-standing desire. Far down the road now he could see a small, moving figure. She had to come; he'd known that all along. While Charity's form grew large and distinguishable, Concho Bill eased his saddle gun from the scabbard and levered a round into the chamber.

Excitement gave him a powerful rush when she came close enough to almost discern her features. Only a little closer. Then she freed one leg from its stirrup and dropped to the side of her horse. No. It looked as though she had bounced free and fallen from the saddle. In that instant, everything stopped going the way Bill Baudine planned it.

*

Fury rode with Charity Rose. A woman she hardly knew had become a victim of Baudine's madness. She had listened with ill-concealed impatience while Joshua made a suggestion. When he finished, she saw some sense in what he said. Forcing the agitation out of her mind, she gave her attention to the sketchily outlined plan.

Her main advantage lay in the gang not knowing that she had learned of the plot in advance. That put time on her side to devise some workable plan to upset Baudine's scheme. One of the more difficult things would be to appear surprised when "official" word of what had happened reached her.

When Baudine's messenger located Charity and her companions in camp along the road from Virginia City, she put on a convincing display. She even threatened to kill the bringer of bad news, before she allowed him to ride off smirking. By then, Grandy had contacted his friends among the Lucky Strike miners—a project delayed by her arrest and escape—and returned to where Charity waited. Joshua scouted the road and, using the directions provided, located the turnoff.

He came to the deadend and nodded in appreciation. It made a perfect ambush site. He felt certain, he reported back to Charity, that the part he and Grandy were to play could be carried off without any problem. At the appointed time, Charity set off on her risky journey. She reached the diverging trail and took it, in the process observing the hardcase make his signal to those waiting ahead. Once out of his sight, she reined in and dismounted.

From items in her saddlebags she quickly assembled a mannequin, which she placed in the saddle. Mounting up behind the dummy, she set off once more toward her terrible destiny. A slight bend obscured the deadend ambush site and Charity used it to advantage. She kicked free of the saddle and gave a slap of her quirt to her mount's rump. That set Lucifer into a gallop.

Exposed now to the weapons of the gang, and unsupported, the dummy began to slip to one side. It fell to the earth a moment before Concho Bill fired his first

193

round. An irregular crash of gunfire followed. A dozen more bullets struck home in the rag-stuffed mannequin. Then came the heavy boom of a Sharps .56. A man gave a short, high yell and fell out from behind a rock. Hot lead came from another direction and the outlaws ducked low to avoid the fate of the first man.

Charity used the lull to come into view and put a round through Concho Bill's coat, close enough to his side to feel its passage. He dropped to the ground and Charity whistled for Lucifer. Obediently the big black came to her. Slugs cracked through the air around as she mounted. Grandy's Sharps went off again and Concho Bill stared unbelievingly while his horse went stiff-legged and fell to one side.

Driven out by the thrashing animal's death throes, Concho Bill found himself vulnerable to the hidden guns above and beyond him. He dodged for a stand of aspen. Charity clipped the heel from one of his boots as he dived into the line of trees. A Bisley in each hand, she spurred Lucifer and streaked away around the bend, free from harm. A ten-minute fast run reunited her with her companions.

"I thought I had him," Charity complained after greeting Josh and Grandy. "There are too many of them for us to have stayed. Grandy, have you heard anything?"

"Ayap. Some of the miners found where Mrs. Foster had been taken. She's safe now and restin' at home. An' there's a couple of yer boy, Baudine's, men warmin' their backsides on the hub of Hell."

"Who rescued her? I'd like to thank them," Charity declared.

"They're new fellers. Sean O'Day and Brian Killabrough. Word is they're some sort of organizers, like I told you before, but I reckon they did a whole lot of disorganizing those fellers out at the diggin's."

"What do we do now?" Joshua asked.

"With Baudine and his men out here, the logical thing is to tear into his operations in town. Is the strike going to happen?" she asked Grandy.

"The minute we ride into Sweetwater," the old-timer assured her.

"Good. We'll give Baudine so much to worry over he won't have time to think about us."

Storm clouds gathered in Concho Bill's smokey eyes. He had taken a horse from one of his men and ridden ahead. He preceded everyone who had been at the canyon. Now his wrath exploded in Frenchy Descoines's office.

"Someone tipped her off. Goddamnit, she isn't a mind-reader, so she had to know in advance about the ambush. That slippery bitch got away again."

Frenchy produced a Gallic shrug. "What does it matter, *mon ami?* There are but three of them. That much we do know. As to your informer, I have an idea who that might be. I'll take care of it later. Now, drink some brandy, sit down, relax."

"I'll relax when I see Charity Rose's corpse stretched out in a coffin."

A soft rap at the door prevented him from enlarging on the idea. "Come," Frenchy invited.

A small boy, Gerd Meeker's son, entered, eyes wide with excitement. "My Paw said to come tell you, there's trouble at the Lucky Strike. The miners have gone on strike."

"What!" Baudine exploded. "Damn that woman.

But . . . how could she be behind this? I'll come back with you, Timmy," he told the lad. "This, if anything, will bring Charity Rose to town. Alert everyone to be watching for her, Frenchy."

Evening had come to Sweetwater, and with it a torchlight parade. Shouting, jeering miners walked through the streets while more blocked off the gateway to the Lucky Strike. At the rooming house where she lived as C. M. Rose, Charity met with Conrad O'Farrel and Brian Killabrough to revise her strategy. Joshua and Grandy listened while they kept watch on the approaches to the building.

"The key to everything is the Tivoli Palace," Charity informed her audience. "While everyone's attention is on the mine strike, that's where we hit next. I learned earlier that one of the girls had been subjected to some sort of torture. That gives me some idea about that dead one we found, Josh. Then, later, I found out this new one was Della Terrace. It was because she sent us warning of the trap Baudine planned. That's another reason for hitting the Tivoli. If we could insure getting the innocent people out, I'd like to burn it to the ground."

"Leave that to the lads from the mine, Miss," Brian Killabrough offered.

"Ummm. Well, then, the first order is to get rid of Burt Kill. He's a little vacant in the head, but he's fast, mean and far too powerful to want to handle in a stand-up fight. I'll handle him; then we go to work on the inside."

"What comes next?" Conrad O'Farrel asked.

"What else? The Lucky Strike. Meeker has sent for strike-breakers. They should be here, some of the early

196

ones, by tomorrow. Within three days they can break the picket line and reopen the mine with new workers. So we take the mine away from Baudine before they can get set up."

"How are you going to handle Burt?" Joshua asked.

"I—ah—" Charity responded, eying Grandy's L. C. Smith, "have an idea worked out."

Business was slow. With those crazy miners on strike, few people felt like celebrating. Although many around the Tivoli Palace lamented this state of affairs, Burt Kill didn't mind at all. It gave him time to go out back for a breath of fresh air and a smoke. Burt felt bad about Mr. Descoines not letting him poke that girl Della they had in the cellar the other day. Burt had not had a poke in a long time.

Burt stopped thinking to concentrate on the intricate operation of making and rolling a cigarette. He had just gotten to the licking part when he heard a noise out in the dark, to the side of the stable house. He stopped and looked up. There, another sound. A loud click. Burt knew what that was.

It was a gun being cocked. Burt dropped his unfinished cigarette and clumsily drew his sixgun. Then Burt caught a severe case of dead when the column of zero-zero buckshot from the L. C. Smith in Charity's hands blew off the top half of his head.

No plan survives first contact with the enemy, Charity thought, back at the rooming house. The idleness at the Tivoli Palace due to the strike had left a lot of Baudine's

197

men with nothing to do. In the seconds after the shotgun blast, they had swarmed out of the huge bordello and begun a search. Charity had managed to evade them only by quick wits and a bit of quiet running. Butch provided several useful distractions, also, by attacking lone gunmen who prowled the neighborhood around the Tivoli Palace.

"Our attack on the Tivoli is off," Charity informed the men waiting in her room. "The place is full of Baudine men." She went on to describe the instant reaction to her killing of Burt, then added, "Your miners might be willing to fight for better working conditions, Conrad, but they don't need to die facing down experienced gunfighters. We have to stir up more confusion."

"But how?" Conrad O'Farrel asked. "We're doin' all we can without forcin' a shootout."

"I've been thinking on it while I made my way back here. By tomorrow the strike-breakers will be in large enough number to be effective. Now here's what I see as the way to twist Concho Bill's tail," Charity began, and talked late into the night.

CHAPTER 19

While the cocks still crowed and breakfast fires sent new smoke into the pale sky, three wagon loads of strike-breakers arrived to join their brothers in Sweetwater. Now some fifty strong, they formed up on the main street and marched in tight ranks toward the Lucky Strike. Pickets had already rushed to take a blockading position across the front fence. With axe handles and gun butts the burly, hard-faced strike-breakers waded into the miners and began to drive them back against the gates. Slowly their number dwindled and the hired toughs wrenched the lock and chain from the barrier and poured onto the mine's property.

More miners arriving at the scene had time only to pound on a few backs as the strike-breakers pushed inside and spread out. Their apparent leader took a couple of cocky strides toward the miners and tilted his chin aggressively. He spoke with a bull bass.

"You men have until tomorrow morning to report to your jobs or you won't have any jobs."

"Dirty scab," shouted a bowlegged miner in the front

rank. "You ain't gonna work the mine. Not a one of ye who knows the meaning of honest labor."

"Aye. Ye'd best be leavin' before some real trouble starts."

"That's what we came here for. You all do as you're told or you'll see the sort of real trouble you never dreamed of," the spokesman riposted.

"Ah, be gone wi' ye," Conrad O'Farrel shouted. "The only one in your family who ever worked was yer mother . . . and she did that on her back."

Brian Killabrough picked up a rock and hurled it at the boss strike-breaker. The burly leader batted the jagged missile out of the way with an axe handle.

"One final warning to you. We're deputized as city policemen. You men come to work or get along somewhere else. If you try to picket the mine, you'll be arrested for loitering and public nuisance. So give up the strike or be gone."

Two long, tense minutes passed, then a disgruntled murmur rose among the miners. They outnumbered the strike-breakers by now, but none save the Molly McGuires were armed. At last they began to drift away. While they strolled down the street toward the unofficial headquarters of the strike, Finnegan's Bucket of Suds, Conrad O'Farrel spoke softly to Brian Killabrough.

"Sure an' I'm thinkin' that lump o' beef is for playin' right into our hands. Won't be no trouble now to stir up a little excitement to draw them gunhawks away from the Tivoli."

"Killabrough knew what he was talking about,"

Charity Rose whispered to Joshua Blaine. "Here they come."

Night had come to Sweetwater after a day of tense, armed vigilance. Waiting in the dark outside Conrad O'Farrel's home, Charity and her companions formed a welcoming committee. Brian Killabrough, the Molly McGuire organizer, had revealed at the afternoon strategy meeting that the strike-breakers would likely use the cover of night to move against the identified strike leaders. Volunteers now waited at the indicated houses to ambush Baudine's hired thugs. The dozen armed, silent men whom Charity saw swing into the street could have only one purpose in mind.

"There's enough of them," Joshua observed. "Will it come to any killing?" he added, a worried note in his voice.

"The idea is to chase them off. I sometimes get the feeling Brian and Liam would like to get some blood shed; their labor organization certainly has that reputation back East. We'll shoot over their heads first. If that fails, shoot to wound."

"And if that doesn't stop them?"

"Josh, we're here to keep them from getting the people they're after. We'll do what we have to."

"But you and I know that none of them are inside."

"True. But those thugs from the mine don't," Charity answered grimly.

Grandy gave a nightbird cry from the other side of the house, where he had gone to get the strike-breakers in a cross-fire. "Grandy's ready," Charity stated.

Two doors down from the O'Farrels' the mine's hoodlums broke into a shuffling run. Axe handles glinted in the moonlight and two men with rifles took up positions to either end of the front line. Charity took aim on one upraised oak shaft and squeezed off a round.

Cursing the pain that surged down his arm, the strike-breaker dropped his shattered weapon. Buckshot tore up a cloud of dust a few feet in front of the attackers. Their shuffling trot faltered. Another load of zero-zero buck halted them.

"There's nothing here you want," Joshua called to the stalled men.

One of the riflemen tried to sight on the voice. Charity shot him in the shoulder. "Goddamn, they got us cold," one strike-breaker declared from the middle of the mob.

Buckshot made a fluttery sound over their heads, like the wings of the angel of death. Four of them, including the wounded man, had had enough. They turned and fled toward the safety of the mine. Charity and Joshua fired over their heads also.

"There's at least three of them," another tough announced.

"Don't make a difference. You can't take on a scattergun with a pick stem. I'm for gettin' out of here."

Like a skittery herd in a thunderstorm, the remaining eight men bolted and ran. Charity sent a couple of random shots after them to hurry the defeated mob. Joshua heaved a long sigh.

"It went better than I thought."

"It's not over yet, Josh," Charity reminded him.

Hardly half an hour passed after the defeat of the squads sent to round up strike leaders before Concho Bill Baudine called an emergency meeting at the mine office.

202

Gerd Meeker wore an anxious expression, as did the boss of the strike-breakers. Concho Bill had a mask of fury and his cold eyes pierced each man in the room.

"There's no question that the next object will be to storm the mine and force concessions out of us."

"Those damned miners," Meeker began, to be cut off by Baudine.

"There's more to it than that. Those miners are being led by agents of the Molly McGuires. I'm certain of that. And Charity Rose has thrown in with them. They'll want a quick end to this, so a direct assault on the mine is the most logical way of getting that. I want all of Buck's men, all of ours," he added for Frenchy Descoines, "to be brought here. Even if they're not crack shots, there are a great deal more miners than there are of us. We'll need every gun we can round up. Besides that," Concho Bill concluded, rising from the table, "I'll have some special surprises set up for when they attack the mine."

Knowledge of the attempts to capture their leaders aroused the miners to a vengeful state far beyond peaceful picketing. Shortly after dawn, the hundred-twenty men gathered in the main street of Sweetwater. There they listened to accounts of the previous night. At the conclusion of this recitation, Brian Killabrough announced the intention of the strikers to march on the mine. Armed and ready to do considerable violence, the miners formed into ranks and set off for the Lucky Strike.

"Here they come, Mr. Holoburton," one of the strike-breaker sentries called out when the miners reached the bottom of the low hill where the Lucky Strike was located.

"Good," Concho Bill gloated. "Let 'em keep coming. Remember, we don't touch off any of the dynamite bombs until they get to the innermost arc. Then we shoot that one, the one at the back, and lastly the middle line. That should take care of the miners."

"I think everyone is looking the proper direction," Charity Rose declared. "Let's get on over to the Tivoli Palace."

Charity, Joshua and Grandy advanced along the boardwalk to the open block of land occupied exclusively by the Tivoli Palace. Each carried a covered wicker picnic basket. Charity wore her mannish clothing. So far they had met no opposition. Grandy went around one side to cover the back, while Charity and Joshua took the graveled path to the front door. Charity gave Grandy a slow count to ten to give him time to get in place. Then she reached out and turned the bell knob.

One of the maids answered the door. "You fellers are kind of early, aren't you?" she asked.

Charity and Joshua pushed on past her into the hallway. There they stopped and Charity spoke to the young cleaning woman. "Get out of here now and don't look back."

"Wha—why?"

"Do as I say and you won't be harmed." She raised her voice to include the six people on the ground floor. "All of you get out of here now. We're going to tear the place down."

No one moved. Charity's drawn sixgun changed two minds and the dusting of furniture ceased. Quickly the determined pair started for the staircase. On the second floor they began knocking on doors and calling for the girls to get dressed and hurry outside.

"Bring everything you have of value, but don't waste a lot of time over clothes," Charity explained to one harlot. "We're going to burn this place to the ground."

"Fire!" a young soiled dove squealed loudly in the hall.

Good idea, Charity thought. "That's right, the place is on fire. Everybody out. Hurry! Fire!"

Doors banged open and a pandemonium of feminine voices filled the inner balcony. Charity started for the stairway to the third floor. Partway up, the first opposition developed. Two hardcases had been kept back by Mattie Orcutt more for her own protection than that of the establishment. When the shouting started, they left Mattie's suite to find out the cause. Side-by-side, they reached the stairs and headed down as Charity looked up and saw them. Her Colt Bisley barked and one gunhawk went down with a slug in his belly.

His partner crouched and drew his own weapon. His shot scarred the wall alongside Charity's head and showered her with plaster dust. Eyes burning, she threw herself forward, thus avoiding the second round that cracked past overhead. Charity fired blindly.

Her bullet hit the wounded man, who discharged his sixgun into the open ceiling of glass. Huge broken shards began the long fall to the ground floor, tinkling musically. Charity triggered her Bisley again. The second outlaw cried out in a thin, high voice and tumbled down the treads toward her. With this respite, Charity took time to wipe at her eyes. Her body's natural defenses had taken over and tears quickly removed the rest of the irritant.

Resistance silenced, Charity started up the stairway once more. On the top floor she could clearly hear Mattie Orcutt's cawing voice from inside the elaborate suite the madam occupied.

"Once they set those bombs off, it'll be over for the miners and we can get some boys back here."

A muttered response came from the unidentified person with her. Charity started that way. Then the importance of what Mattie had said reached her. Some sort of bombs that would wipe out the striking miners. Immediately she started back for the stairwell. Della Terrace and Wesley, the towel boy, emerged from one room and Charity gestured to them.

Quickly she outlined what she had overheard and urged them to hurry to find Conrad O'Farrel and Brian Killabrough. "Tell them about the bombs. Hurry, don't let them get too close to the mine."

With them sped off on their errand, Charity headed back to Mattie's suite. She swung wide the open door and stepped inside.

Mattie flew off the edge of the bed, a fanged and clawed harpy and came at Charity so fast that the young bounty hunter had barely time to holster her revolver. Mattie went for her eyes.

Charity dodged to one side, grabbed two handsful of Mattie's hennaed hair, and yanked. Mattie went down in a tangle of skirt and legs, screeching obscenities at her tormentor. Charity dropped astraddle Mattie's waist and began to punish her face with hard fists. Mattie bucked and flopped like an unbroken horse. With one mighty heave, she dislodged Charity and sent her sprawling.

Moving remarkably fast for a woman of her bulk, Mattie scrambled after Charity and managed to wrap arms around her waist. The enraged madam flung Charity from side to side in her powerful grasp, then hurled her toward the wall. Legs cocked up nearly to her chin, Charity slammed out at the last minute, breaking the force of her contact with the plaster. She rebounded and came upright in time to see Mattie scramble across the floor to a dressing table in one corner.

The rotund madam pulled herself upright and picked up a hand mirror. This she flung at Charity, followed by a comb, brush, a pot of lip rouge, and lastly an open, tortoiseshell container of face powder. A pearlescent cloud enveloped the room in its wake. Charity ducked or batted away each object. She could barely see through the haze of face powder. Mattie's bulk moved and Charity braced herself.

Howling like a demented beast, Mattie launched herself at Charity, a knife with a long, thin, wicked blade upraised to strike. Only four paces separated them and Charity barely managed to pivot out of the way. Swiftly she grasped the wrist of Mattie's knife hand. Biting her lower lip, Charity wrenched on the extended wrist and flung Mattie away. Window glass tinkled and Mattie shrieked in agony. She turned to face Charity with blood streaming down her face.

To Charity's keen disappointment, Mattie had not lost her grip on the knife. She charged again, slashing the air with the terrible sharp edge. Charity ducked and had to roll to one side. Giving a shout of triumph, Mattie bounded after her. Her back against the wall, hemmed in by an armoire and the dressing table, Charity had no route of escape. The knife blade flashed in the morning sun that spilled in the ruined window. Another foot and the blade would slide into her flesh.

"Now you'll get yours," Mattie gloated.

With a reluctant little sigh, Charity pulled her left-hand Colt Bisley and put a .45 slug through the middle of Mattie's heart. The stout madam tottered a moment, then swayed into a backbend that ended with the bleeding top of her head pressed to the floor. A long, low moan came from deep in her chest and she toppled to one side.

Charity opened one bottle of kerosene from the hamper and began to sprinkle it around the room.

CHAPTER 20

Sweetwater's main street had been turned into a battleground. A hundred angry miners could burn a lot of gunpowder. Thick layers of smoke hung over the far end of the street, where the hill rose to the Lucky Strike mine. Tipped off by Charity Rose about the landmines, Brian Killabrough and Conrad O'Farrel halted the miners short of the suspected area. From there they laid down a steady volume of fire that sent bullets ripping through the flimsy walls of the office and mine head.

For all their prowess with firearms, the strike-breakers had been forced to lie low. Within twenty minutes of the initial assault, the battle degenerated into occasional sniping. When Frenchy Descoines managed to escape from the beleaguered Tivoli Palace and flee to the mine in considerable panic, the sharpshooters among the miners gave him more reason for haste. One carpetbag he carried, loaded with paper currency, was shot from his hand. It landed hard and snapped the lock.

A random breeze sprang up for a moment and scattered money all over the ground. Several miners threw off caution and sported among the ill-gotten gains until one fell dead from a strike-breaker's Winchester round and the others scurried for safety. Still, the strikers refused to move forward, and Concho Bill Baudine cursed their stubbornness. Meanwhile, Charity and her companions drove everyone from the Tivoli Palace.

From the higher ground of the Lucky Strike, Baudine and his partner watched helplessly. Gamblers, bartenders and painted ladies spilled out onto the yard around the three-story structure. Twice the muffled sounds of gunshots came from inside. Then the sight they both dreaded became reality.

With an effect much like heat waves on the desert, the upper floor of the Tivoli Palace began to waver in the distorted air. Then flames licked from one window. A moment later, more fire appeared on the second floor. Frenchy Descoines groaned aloud and made as though he would rush there to prevent the destruction. He stopped after a single, faltering step. Hungry red tongues flickered on the ground floor.

White at first, a huge column of smoke formed and rose from the doomed building. It roiled and twisted in the heated air, going from white to gray and then black as the all-consuming conflagration ate away at the expensive furnishings, drapes and polish-saturated woodwork. Rapid-fire pops sounded as liquor bottles exploded. Frenchy groaned again and covered his eyes with his long fingers. Concho Bill cursed in a continuing, scathing stream. The crowd in the yard retreated from the tremendous heat.

From their midst came three persons. Concho Bill had no need of field glasses to know that one of these had to be Charity Rose. People along the street joined them.

210

Purposefully they advanced on the mine.

"Granger, get some of your men and go down there."

"How do I get around those miners?"

"Go around the side, idiot. They're all concentrated to our front because of the dynamite," Baudine growled.

Quickly the chief of police and four officers departed to do Baudine's bidding.

They reached the main street in time to get between the miners and the reinforcements. Wade Granger stepped ahead of his underlings and raised a hand to halt the procession. "Go about your business, folks. The trouble at the mine is being taken care of."

"I have reason to believe Concho Bill Baudine and Frenchy Descoines are up there, and I intend to capture them," Charity informed the lawman.

"You are a fugitive. It was a stupid move to come back to town. You and the men next to you are all under arrest."

"You can't make it stick, Chief," Charity challenged.

"I think I can," Granger growled as he drew his sixgun.

Granger's revolver had barely cleared leather when a bullet ripped through the sleeve of his thick shirt, grazing his arm. Grunting, he went to his knees. His officers opened fire and a steady rattle of shots cut them down. In the brief flurry of action, Wade Granger managed to dodge between two buildings and make his way back to the Lucky Strike.

"After him," Charity commanded.

"They've figured out that there're no explosives to the sides," Wade Granger panted as he clambered over the

211

low fence and onto Lucky Strike land.

"What do you mean?" Concho Bill demanded.

"They're right behind me." Granger started an uneven shuffle away from his boss.

"Where do you think you're going?" Baudine demanded.

"Away from here. The whole thing is collapsing; you can see that. I'm going to save myself while I can."

Concho Bill started a scathing reply, to be cut off by a terrific series of blasts. One of the strike-breakers had taken over on the fuse trains and had set off one chain of landmines. Mouthing a foul curse, Concho Bill started toward the mine office.

On the way, he looked to the south along the street and saw the miners rise up and begin a rush. They advanced, firing, beyond the craters made by the first string of explosions. Then, like trained troops, they flopped down at a barked command. The second line of bombs went off in a staggered blast. From behind him, Baudine heard the sound of more miners advancing along the route used by Wade Granger. He broke into a run that carried him to the office and inside.

"Frenchy, come on. They're going to be here in a minute. That damned Charity Rose is with them. We've got to run for it."

Shouts of alarm came from outside. Concho Bill and Frenchy made undignified exits through a window. They were joined by Wade Granger, Sergeant Bleaker, Gerd Meeker and Buck Harris. The horses of some late arrivals remained unsaddled near the mine. Baudine and those with him grabbed up reins, mounted and rode off, leaving their underlings to what fate might provide them.

*　　　*　　　*

Gathering horses and setting off in pursuit cost Charity and Joshua a critical half hour. Sweetwater was in turmoil, and clearing the streets enough to get through consumed most of that. At least, Charity soon found, Concho Bill had made no effort to conceal his trail. The six fugitives had rounded town, splashed through Sweetwater Creek and headed north toward Virginia City.

Exactly what Charity had anticipated in the event of a breakout. Now if Marshal Donovan did his part, Concho Bill would be caught between those hunting him. The ground grew steeper as they progressed. From the length of stride, the horses ridden by the fugitives would be tiring soon. Despite the long lead Baudine had, Charity kept the pace slower. Joshua complained about their easy gait.

"It's not the fastest horse in the morning that counts, Josh," she told him. "It's the one that's still going by evening."

They rode on, twenty miles rolling away under their horses' hoofs. Some five miles out of Virginia City they came upon a sudden change in the sign they followed.

"Heading west," Charity announced. "We saw where they slowed their mounts. Now they've set off at a gallop again. Looks like Concho Bill saw Marshal Donovan's posse before they saw him. They're headed for the Sierra Nevada."

Gradually the terrain changed from high desert to mountains. Conifers and aspen replaced cactus and cottonwood. Here and there ancient, gnarled live oaks dotted the boulder-strewn foothills. The still-clear trail led toward a towering pair of peaks that marked the route of the ill-fated Donner party.

"Looks like Concho Bill is expecting to find safety in

California," Charity speculated.

"That's a long trip," Joshua remarked. "Especially this late in fall. There's snow up there now. That's—ah, what happened to the Donners."

"If they don't ease up on those horses, or get remounts, they'll be on foot before long."

"Then what?" Joshua asked.

"Marshal Donovan catches them, or we do."

Jays scolded and crows made raucous cawing among the dropping leaves of scarlet, brown and gold. Concho Bill Baudine had been observing the small Butterfield stage relay station for ten minutes he begrudged to the task. Their horses wouldn't make it farther. Not with at least two posses on their trail.

They had barely avoided the marshal's hunters from Virginia City. It could be no one else. And since she was alive, Charity Rose would be hot after him, too. Would there be more? It didn't matter. Only two people tended the station. An old man and a boy in his teens. Easy enough. Concho Bill rose and returned to the others.

"We gonna ride down there and take them horses, uh, Bill?" Wade Granger asked, uncomfortable with the new name.

"No-o-o. That could end in some killing. Right now we don't need that. Stage lines are notorious for low pay. I think we can go in there and trade for fresh mounts, and spread around a little money and get the posse off our trail for good."

"How do we do that?" Bleaker asked.

"We take our time leaving. We'll buy silence from the station agents, then pull a drag after us, use the main trail

214

for a while, then branch off."

"Sounds good," Gerd Meeker said with forced cheerfulness.

"It had better be, or we could swing on the gallows," Concho Bill reminded them.

Charity and Joshua found part of Marshal Donovan's posse at the Butterfield relay station. They had already developed a holiday spirit, grateful to be out of the hard riding and potential danger of flying bullets. They drank and played cards, uncaring whether a handful of outlaws escaped or not. They would be less than useless, Charity and Joshua quickly agreed. These culls could at least provide information, Charity hoped.

"They changed horses here," one of the more sober possemen told her, "then took off along the main road, pulling a drag. The Butterfield agent told us that much. Marshal Donovan and twenty men went on. We're supposed to rest our mounts and come along later with fresh horses for them that rode ahead."

Not wanting to lose any time, Charity and Joshua set off at a brisk canter. The grade steepened abruptly, causing Lucifer and Joshua's horse to snort and grunt as they labored uphill. Charity kept her eyes on the irregular marks made by the drag and the hoofprints that overlaid them. Well out of sight of the stage station, beyond a large, curving buttress of mountain flank, she discovered a barely discernable discrepancy. Rounded depressions appeared in a large delta formation of crumbled decomposed granite.

Reining in, Charity studied them closely. They led away toward another, secondary pass through the range.

215

Enough of the faint spore existed to account for six men, she reasoned. Yet, the drag continued along with the sign of the marshal's posse.

"They took along one or more spare horses to pull the drag," Charity stated confidently. "Which means the Butterfield employees didn't tell all about Concho Bill's stopover. They must have been paid for silence."

"Only not enough by their lights to be completely silent, eh?" Joshua offered.

"Exactly. Now it's up to us to figure out where Baudine's leading them and why."

Continuous, the crash and rumble of tons of water falling down the sheer face drowned out any reasonable conversation. It became necessary to communicate by signs and shouts. Much to the horror of their underlings, Concho Bill Baudine and Frenchy Descoines found themselves in a box canyon, at the head of which a tremendous, towering waterfall hissed and seethed and roared. At once Meeker, Granger and Bleaker wanted to turn back. Buck Harris looked at them scornfully.

"And ride into that fucking posse?"

"Buck's right," Concho Bill shouted close to Meeker's ear. "They may be dumb enough to follow the drag for a long ways, but eventually those horses will play out or stop to graze and the marshal will know what happened. It'll be hard, but he'll find where we left the road. Then there's Charity Rose."

"Shit, Bill," Meeker countered. "She's only a woman."

"Yeah, and she brought us to this. I, for one, don't want to stay here and face her. There has to be a way up

216

that cliff face, even though we'll have to leave the horses behind. It won't matter. No one else can get their mounts out of here except by going the long way around."

"Bill's right," Buck added support. "Spread out and look for a way."

It took less than a quarter hour. Rugged boulders, spray damp and worn down by erosion, formed a sort of staircase to one side of the falls. Buck Harris and Wade Granger had found a steep, precipitous slope that might be negotiated by a horse in desperation. The others rejected that alternative out of hand.

"Then we had better start climbing," Frenchy suggested. "If I'm not mistaken, that's the point of the posse." He pointed down the canyon to where two mounted figures could be seen coming fast.

Swiftly they began to work their way up the rocks. Concho Bill, in the lead, had made less than fifty feet when rock chips exploded close by his face, showering him with jagged shards. Blood began to seep from half a dozen cuts. More slugs began to moan and whine off the bounders.

"There they are," Joshua called out. "You were right, this was a deadend."

"We can't let them get away," Charity urged, drawing her Winchester from the saddle scabbard.

She fired two quick rounds at the figure farthest up the side of the falls. They had little effect. Then Charity learned an unfriendly lesson. Even in desperate retreat, Concho Bill had laid a plan. It came clear to Charity and Joshua when answering fire came from the screen of gorse near the foot of the falls. Buck Harris and Gerd

217

Meeker formed a rear guard that drove the avengers to cover.

Charity landed behind a boulder and motioned Joshua to remain where he sheltered behind a tall, rough-barked pine. Carefully she ghosted to one side, eyes on the next point of cover she could reach with a short rush. She paused at a boulder, rose and levered through two rounds. With the enemies' heads down, she ran to her next position.

Her movement drew Buck Harris's attention and he opened fire, only to be driven to the ground by Joshua's covering shots. Charity moved again. She continued the action until she had a clear view of the two men of the rear guard. She took careful aim and shot Gerd Meeker through the left thigh.

He dropped his rifle and howled in agony, clutching his wounded limb. Buck Harris threw a wild shot and ran to a niche closer to the falls. He had nearly sunk out of sight when Charity's .44-40 round took him under the left arm and tore through his chest. He fell dead with the back of his head in a whirlpool of bubbles, staining them bright pink. All that remained now was to stop the others.

CHAPTER 21

Forcing a bellow, Chief Granger called above to Concho Bill. "They got Harris and Meeker."

"Keep climbing," Baudine panted back.

From below, Charity shifted her attention off the dead men to the four who struggled up the sheer cliff face. Taking her time, she drew a bead on the closest one. With a gentle, continuous pressure she squeezed the trigger. The Winchester cracked and recoiled sharply against her shoulder.

Her slug took Sergeant Bleaker in the right hip. One moment he held on to a pointed rock for support. The next he let go in reaction to the bullet impact and wavered in a frantic effort to recover his balance. His weight came on his right leg and his hip gave way. He leaned away from the security of the boulders in graceful slow motion, and began to fall. He screamed in terror all the way to the bottom of the fall, where he disappeared under the water.

"I'm going after them," Charity shouted to Joshua. "Stay and watch the front door."

"No, Charity. Don't!"

His appeal came too late. No longer menaced by gunfire, Charity ran to the base of the fall and studied the ascent. She couldn't catch them in time that way, and she had no means of taking along sufficient firepower. Off to one side she saw the horses tethered at the base of a rotting slope of decomposed granite. Quickly she ran there and examined the slope.

It looked shaky, but possible. Behind her, heard through the thunder of the falls like a child's cork gun, Joshua continued to fire at the climbing outlaws. Charity retrieved Lucifer and walked him to the precipitous slope. She scabbarded her Winchester and swung into the saddle.

"Let's go, boy. You can do it."

Grunting and snorting in protest, Lucifer began the strenuous climb.

Another seventy-five feet, Concho Bill Baudine estimated as muscles that burned and ached strained to draw him another small increment up the side of the tumult of water that cascaded past his right side. His hand closed on another point of rock and he heaved, only to have his grip slide away to nothingness. He dropped hard onto the ledge where he had started two punishing handholds before. Cursing, he maneuvered himself to a better position and forged on.

"Goddamnit, they're still shooting at us," Chief Granger howled.

"I know," Frenchy said from above him. "Watch where you grab. Don't look back at them."

Shards from a bullet impact rattled against Frenchy's coat. He bit his lower lip and forced himself to take another slow, cautious movement upward. Below him, Wade Granger risked another backward glance. Joshua Blaine stood in the open, firing with ease. A slight movement to one side of the young prospector attracted Granger's attention. He never heard the shot, but saw the puff of smoke. Blaine's rifle went flying and he fell to the ground.

Good enough, Granger thought. Even though wounded, Gerd Meeker had managed to put some of the opposition out of action. The pudgy mining engineer had more courage than he had thought. Maybe they would get out of this after all. Then he grabbed the same wrong point of rock Baudine had taken hold of. His grip failed and he fell to the ledge.

"Ow! Damn," Wade Granger yelled as pain surged in his twisted ankle. "Bill, hey, Bill, I sprained my ankle."

"Too bad. We can't carry you," Baudine shouted back. "Frenchy's got a rope along. Keep 'em off us from there and we'll drop it down to you when we get on top."

Relieved, if not entirely credulous, Wade Granger waved his companions on. He looked back and saw that Joshua had not moved. Where was that damned woman?

Exhausted and sopping wet, Concho Bill Baudine and Frenchy Descoines dragged themselves over the rough lip of the canyon wall. For long moments they lay staring at the sky, panting and shivering in the cool mountain air. At last Concho Bill rolled onto his belly and came to his knees. He raised his head to see the spread-legged

221

form of Charity Rose, holding a cocked Colt Bisley on him. Caught cold, Baudine could do nothing but raise his hands. Beside him, Frenchy did the same.

"H-how did you get up here?" Concho Bill panted out.

"It wasn't easy," Charity answered him.

Lucifer had fallen to his haunches twice on the tortuous climb. Pink froth filled the black's mouth from the chafing of the bit. It had taken every ounce of the valiant horse's stamina to complete the climb. Charity had dismounted and patted his neck, then cooed reassurances in one ear. Then she had headed for the top of the falls. Concho Bill and Frenchy had arrived only an instant ahead of her. Now she had to finish the job.

"I never believed it would end like this. You both look like drowned rats. I'm going to take great pleasure out of turning you both over to the law and watching you hang. I once thought I'd kill you with my own hands. But that would be too quick. Waiting for the hangman will give you time to think."

Concho Bill looked at her with horror-filled eyes. Gone was the hatred and contempt; only naked fear remained. Suddenly she staggered and fell to one side. The roar of the falls had hidden the sound of a gunshot, Baudine realized a moment later when the head of Wade Granger appeared over the lip. Sixgun leading the way, the former chief of police forced himself onto the bank of the stream that fed the falls. Gasping, he got to his knees, then stood upright.

"Go-got to finish it," he panted, advancing on Charity Rose.

Bisley tightly gripped with both hands, her mind struggling to fight off pain, Charity eared back the hammer and fired. Her bullet struck Wade Granger in the chest, nicking a corner of his heart and rupturing the pulmonary artery. A startled expression washed over Granger's face. Groaning softly, he staggered backward and disappeared over the falls.

Their minds on escape only, Concho Bill and Frenchy did not stay to watch the end of their courageous underling. They set off at a shambling run. Quickly conscious of this, Charity turned on the ground and triggered another round before she passed out.

Once more, she thought as darkness descended, Baudine had escaped her. She never knew that he carried with him a bitter memento. A bullet-shattered kneecap would make him limp stiff-leggedly the rest of his life.

Sunlight made warm spots of her closed eyelids. Moaning, Charity opened her eyes to see Joshua Blaine and Grandy Spears bending over her. Joshua had one shoulder crudely bandaged.

"Take it easy, Charity," Joshua urged. "You took a bad one."

"Josh, you—you're wounded."

"Not too nasty. Grandy came along after us, with some of Conrad O'Farrel's friends. He found me, patched me up, and we came looking for you. I was afraid you'd been—been—well—killed."

"I'm too mean to die, Josh," Charity quipped. "Baudine?"

"Got away. He left a trail of blood, but there's no one to follow. All of our horses are below the falls. The important thing is to get you patched up and to a doctor."

223

"Yes. I agree." Strangely, Charity felt an uncommon sense of peace. Baudine may have gotten away, but she'd taken a piece of him in the process.

"We'll have all the time we need to recuperate together," Joshua promised her.

An imp awakened in Charity's eyes. "I certainly hope it's in a large, comfortable goose-down bed."